'Glades Boy

A Historical Christian Novel
by T. Marie Smith

Foreword by Al Taylor

Cover illustration by T. Marie Smith

WestBow Press books may be ordered through booksellers or by contacting:

WestBow Press
A Division of Thomas Nelson
1663 Liberty Drive
Bloomington, IN 47403
www.westbowpress.com
1-(866) 928-1240

ISBN: 978-1-4497-0526-8 (sc)
ISBN: 978-1-4497-0527-5 (dj)
ISBN: 978-1-4497-0525-1 (e)

Library of Congress Control Number: 2010935757

Cover Art by T. Marie Smith

Printed in the United States of America

WestBow Press rev. date: 10/5/2010

Dedication

I LOVINGLY DEDICATE **'GLADES BOY** TO my terrific husband, Gene, who has given me the freedom to spend time with my writing without complaining, and then served as an expert proofreader and critic.

I also dedicate **'Glades Boy** to my four wonderful children and to each of my thirteen grandchildren in the hope that they will be reminded—*life's crutches, whether alcohol or drugs,* are only debilitating, temporary, and deceiving ***fixes*** that will give **no peace—but God** will never fail. He said, *"Whosoever shall call upon the name of the Lord shall be saved."* Romans 10:13-b

Contents

Foreword

T. MARIE SMITH IS ONE OF those individuals who is blessed with unusual creative skills. She has been highly productive in graphic design for many years. Readers will be delighted that she has now applied her creativity to write a suspenseful and engaging novel. 'GLADES BOY is the profound result of a wonderfully creative mind at work. I am honored that I was asked to write the foreword.

A well written novel can accomplish many things. First of all it must be entertaining. Marie has met that requirement in amazing fashion. From the first page forward, the story moves rapidly through suspenseful circumstances which seem so true-to-life until one wonders if this is perhaps actual history of a person whose life required him to live on the edge of trouble.

The story's setting is found in south Florida in the early 1900's – long before Florida became a tourist attraction. It was a frontier area then and just as rough as the western frontier which has inspired so many novels. The Seminole Indians, who were never subdued because they were immensely skillful at survival in the swamps of the Everglades, were now peaceful neighbors to the settlers. Their knowledge of the environment produced many opportunities to assist those who were ignorant of the "glades". Some of them had also embraced the Christian faith and recognized that this was the grandest thing brought by the settlers. Life was hard. Money was scarce. Society was barely tamed by civilization. Law enforcement was challenged. Outlaws roamed the land robbing, raping, and killing. The Everglades still had plenty of wildlife. Many of the wild animals were capable of killing humans. Those risks added to the suspense of living in the Florida interior swamplands. Difficult circumstances brilliantly highlight the value, the priority, and the comfort of family. The author beautifully develops that powerful truth. The frontier challenges to life seem to clearly show that truth is not a luxury.

A well written novel can also be informative. When history is accurately depicted, the reader finds that this is a good way to become informed while being entertained. Family is also the product of true love stories and love stories at their best are the product of family. Marie gives us a beautiful account of a pretty Indian girl named Io and Zack, the central figure in the novel as their love develops. Romance carries its own suspense and intrigue as it grows. The relationship of these two teenagers and their families demonstrates mutual blessings for those who eschew racism for the ugly thing that it is.

Finally, the author has woven into this novel the paramount place for God in our lives. Zack moved slowly in his quest for spiritual peace, but he found the relationship that he needed through prayer and the influence of those around him who lived for Christ.

This book is entertaining, instructive, and inspiring. I recommend it to you.

Al Taylor

Chapter One

Night Train

The evening air was heavy. Sweltering humidity intensified the pungent stench of swamp vapors. Heat lightning played in the distant sky as Zack stepped up beside his father. Noticing that he was almost as tall as Pa, Zack straightened his shoulders as they walked toward the country store, tavern, and stables that the locals called "town." Osceola Cypress Company had built the logging rail across the road from the stores. The dirt road was dry, and each step kicked up a fine, stifling powder.

It was Saturday evening, and they had just left the rail car that Osceola Company used as an office. The paymaster was gruff but always fair with the loggers.

"Are you going with me tonight, Zack?"

Zack took a deep breath. "Don't reckon so, Pa. I lost almost five dollars in Hawkeye Jacks' game last payday. I promised Ma I'd bring home enough money to help put the roof back on the barn."

He kicked a small rock into a rut as they rounded the last curve.

Two horses were tied up at the hitching rail in front of Hawkeye Jack's Tavern. Zack recognized the 'paint' as belonging to Big John, a black logger who Pa never liked nor trusted. He always suspected him of cheating, although he had never openly accused him. Big

John bragged that he had won the beautiful brown-and-white horse from an Indian in a game of dice, but the Indian had not been seen since that game. Pa said that he was almost sure that Big John had robbed and killed the old Indian.

"Sure hope we don't have another hurricane this year. It's gonna take a lot of work and money to repair all the damage the last one done."

"Did," Pa corrected. "By the way, we'll plan to go home next Saturday. We need to check on your mother and the children."

William Bentley was an educated man but his education did little good for the family as he gambled and drank away almost every penny he could earn.

They went to the store where William bought cigars and matches. "Don't rightly know how late I'll be, so if you change your mind…" biting the tip off one of the cigars and spitting it into the spittoon at the end of the counter, "…you know where I'll be."

Zack looked around the store for a couple of minutes, trying to force himself to go straight to the camp. He purchased a pouch of tobacco and a pack of papers, and then stepped onto the porch. Fighting an urge to go to the tavern, he headed toward the logging camp. Glancing back, he watched Pa disappear into the bar and a crushing sense of loneliness gripped him. Turning sharply, he walked toward Hawkeye's.

"I'm *not* gonna get drunk tonight," he promised himself aloud. "I have to save my money. I'll just have one drink before I go back to camp."

Since the logger's rule was, if you're old enough to saw logs, you're old enough to drink, his rights were never challenged. Besides that, Pa often brewed moonshine at home, and as far back as Zack could remember, he was allowed to drink as much as he wanted. Now, sitting alone, he hated himself because he had sworn many times that he would never be like Pa.

The smell of smoke and the sound of an old player piano filled the air as Zack ordered a drink. Feeling more alone than before, he drank another…then another and another until he forgot he was alone. Finally, purchasing a fifth, he slowly made his way out the door and started back toward camp.

He placed his feet ever so carefully, lifting them higher than necessary, and walking slowly.

"See," he mumbled, "I ain't drunk. I can walk as good as anybody!" Smiling, he held his bottle at arm's length with both hands, as if it were a trophy.

Since daybreak he and Pa had been pulling a crosscut saw in the treacherous cypress swamps. At times the water reached his armpits as he struggled to keep his feet firmly planted under him. He thought about the deadly water moccasins that had been swimming around him before slithering into hiding. Even more frightening was the nesting nine or ten-foot alligator that had silently slipped into the murky water just a few yards from them, but he knew better than to let Pa know that his pounding heart had almost choked him with fear.

Now he was well on the way to forgetting the wretched but familiar daily routine. Walking several hundred yards from the tavern, he reached the edge of high overgrowth and sat on a familiar stump. He had come here often, sometimes to think, sometimes to drink. Again he pulled the cork from his bottle. Tipping his head back, he held the brown glass tightly to his lips and let the fiery liquid fill his mouth. A few drops escaped to trickle down his chin, burning a fresh scratch he had received in the swamp that afternoon.

He had no idea how long he had been sitting there, drinking and smoking.

Thoughts of Io, the most beautiful Indian girl he had ever seen, ran across his mind. Zack had been allowed to go to school for three months in the fifth grade. There he met Io and they had liked each other ever since.

"Io is a very good girl," Zack said as though speaking to the bottle. He envisioned her small frame adorned in a full gathered skirt with brilliantly colored handmade patterns.

Zack remembered when they had first met. He had asked her what *'Io'* meant.

"It's not an Indian name, Zack, but it means *butterfly*." He could almost hear her velvety voice as he recalled her words.

"When my mother was a young girl, a missionary that we called Miss Mary, came to work with the Seminoles. One day a butterfly fluttered by and Miss Mary said 'Io.' She had been a missionary in Africa, and that is where my name came from."

Io had given her life to Jesus as a child, and had tried very hard to help Zack overcome his bad habits. She was tearful when Zack told her he had to go logging with Pa again.

He finished his cigarette and thought about joining Pa and some of his friends in the back room of the tavern where they were drinking and playing poker. On second thought, not wanting to be subjected to Pa's odious disposition, he decided to go to the campsite instead. Besides that, his mind was getting foggy and he knew he should go on to the camp. Since it was Saturday night, he figured a few of the older men would be chatting and playing cards around a dying campfire. Tomorrow he could sleep all day if he so chose.

Now, he no longer cared that he was staggering alone, miles from his home and family, and still a half-mile from the logging camp.

The bottle was empty as was his tobacco pouch.

As he turned to cross the railroad track, his unsure foot slipped on the loose gravel bed and he fell. His face hit the hard metal rail causing severe pain. The empty bottle shattered, leaving the broken bottleneck in his tight grip. He felt warm trickles of blood pouring from his nose and mouth.

Zack ran his tongue across a very painful lip and felt a sharp point on his left front tooth. He realized he had just chipped it.

After a moment he struggled to get to his feet but fell again, his arm landing on a large piece of broken glass. Glancing at his slashed, bloody sleeve, he tried again to stand. Finally he stood, and spread his trembling legs for better balance. Giddily he laughed at himself, thinking how funny he must have looked sprawled across the tracks.

Dizziness filled his head. Falling again between the tracks, he was content to lie there on the sharp gravel and rough wood cross-ties. He relaxed, feeling the world spinning around him.

Suddenly he felt a rumble in the ground underneath him and reached his hand onto one of the tracks. The vibrations told him that if he stayed there, he would be killed. Terror gripped his chaotic mind.

He shook his head trying to clear his vision as he raised himself on one elbow and stared down the tracks. Through the darkness and dense fog, Zack managed to make out the faint outline of a log train coming slowly around the curve.

"Where's the circling headlamp?" his foggy mind questioned.

Confused, he tried once more to get to his feet – once more, with heart pounding and head spinning he fell between the tracks. The rumble grew louder and the vibrations became stronger. Realizing he had to act quickly he began to crawl. Though his head spun he *was* making a little progress. Now the rumble had become a clopping-clatter, violently shaking the ground as the deadly train loomed ever closer. He *had* to get off the tracks! With one track to cross, he decided to try to roll over the formidable steel. Putting all his strength into one final effort, he cried out in terror, "God, help me!"

Zack forced himself across the deadly rail, onto the graveled slope, just as the caboose passed, missing him by inches! Scooting a little further away from the terrifying tonnage, he felt the wind as the passing cars blew tall, sooty grasses around his face. For a few moments he lay frozen with fear on the quivering rocky grade.

"D'ya reckon God *really* heard me?" he wondered aloud.

The empty train moved on past. For some time he lay face down on the sharp gravel and weeds, fading in and out of a drunken stupor.

A faint tinge of dawn was showing on the horizon as Zack opened his eyes. At first he thought he'd had a horrible nightmare, but feeling sharp pain in his face and arm, seeing blood on his clothes and feeling the dried crust of blood on his face as he brushed away bits of gravel and weeds, reality gripped him. Zack weakly wobbled to his feet and grabbed his thighs, hoping to stop the violent trembling.

Trying to put the incident into proper perspective he suddenly remembered the caboose.

Of course! The caboose! There ***is*** *no circling light on a caboose,* he remembered, *neither is there a flagman. They always* ***backed*** *the train into the swamp in the early morning hours, so the cars would be in place to load logs onto them the next day.*

Gathering his wits, Zack straightened himself and ran his fingers through curly black hair, flicking out stems of dried grass and small gravel that had lodged there.

Zack vividly recalled crying to God to help him get off the tracks.

"God, did you really hear me?" he whispered as he rolled his eyes upward.

He remembered the many times Injun Billy Joe had told him that if he ever needed help that he should call on God.

"Injun Billy Joe is more of a father to me than William Bentley ever was." Zack spoke aloud as though the tall, sharp blades of chest-high saw grass could hear.

Through the years, Billy Joe had helped, giving encouragement, instruction, advice and many times, hard labor when it was needed.

Pa was almost never around to do any thing to help, Zack thought bitterly. For years, he had depended on the wisdom of this caring Seminole friend.

Zack stood still for a moment as the eastern sky was miraculously splashed with brilliant pink, yellow and light blue hues across the pleasant Florida dawning. He recalled Injun Billy Joe's deep, clear voice as he said, *"Zack, God will never fail you."*

A Bible verse that he memorized as a child, flashed across his mind. Jesus said, *Call upon me and I will answer.* Could it have truly been that simple?

Fighting waves of nausea and wobbly legs, Zack finally reached the silent campsite.

Chapter Two

Trouble Brewing

Knowing they were to go home for a few days, Zack was glad Saturday had finally arrived. He missed Ma and the young'uns, and could almost feel Harmony Belle's chubby little hands on his face as she welcomed him home.

"Pull that saw," Pa barked.

Zack realized he had been slacking.

He put all his muscle and effort into the crosscut saw as it tore through the wood. A shower of sawdust and the pungent odor of fresh-cut cypress, as well as his aching body, told him they would soon be through another monstrous tree. After a couple more pulls, Zack moved to the safe side of the tree and backed away as Pa's axe cut a wedge out of the opposite side of the mammoth cypress. He then laid a muscular shoulder against the huge trunk.

"*Timmm-berrrr.*" Pa's booming voice echoed through the dense swamp. Zack heard the sharp cracks of dozens of small limbs breaking as they hit nearby trees, followed by the snaps of the thin, un-sawn, woody strands of the falling cypress as they broke. A couple of seconds later, the cypress made contact with a determined thud and the ground trembled beneath him.

They had worked fairly close to the log train most of the week. Zack welcomed staying out of the dangerous, varmint-filled water, but every time he saw the log train, his mind flooded with all the *what ifs* from his terrifying experience last Saturday night. He had not mentioned his near-death experience to anyone, but before going to sleep each night he thanked God for helping him.

After gathering their tools, Zack and Pa walked onto the dusty road and headed to town. Zack made a couple of quick steps to catch up and walk beside with his father.

"I shore will be glad t' see Ma and the young'uns." Zack waited for a response that didn't come, before continuing.

"Wish we could stay home long enough t' fix up the homestead. I reckon a lot needs t' be repaired. With our pay from last week and this week we ought to be able to get most of the supplies we need."

Pa's silence began to make Zack uneasy, but he continued. "I guess Ma's gonna want me t' take her and the young'uns to hear Parson Smith preach Sunday. I think this is the week he comes to Clewist-"

"Zack," Pa interrupted. His cold and quietly deliberate voice stopped Zack dead still. "I lost all my money last Saturday night, and I caught Big John cheating." Pa pulled a big cigar from his shirt pocket before resuming. "Of course he denied it. I saw him dealing my cards from the bottom of the deck, but I couldn't prove it."

Zack caught a quick, knowing breath.

Pa stood still as he bit the end off the cigar, spitting it into the tall grass. He struck a match on the bottom of his boot, and then drew deeply, pulling the flame into the tobacco. After slowly and deliberately puffing three small clouds of smoke into the murky June air, Pa continued.

"I'm going back to Hawkeye's tonight to get my money back."

A cold shiver ran through Zack as they resumed walking. "Guess we won't be going home just yet, will we Pa?" Zack spoke with resignation.

Slowly Zack turned to go to the livery stable. Hearing Pa's boots *clop-clop* in slow defiance on the wooden porch in front of Hawkeye's, he knew he would have to be ready to move at a moment's notice. A sick feeling started in his throat and landed like hot lead in his belly.

Ben, the stable keeper, had leaned his chair against the wall and was snoring as Zack entered the stable. Zack went straight to his horse, Betsy, and began to put the second-hand saddle over the blanket he had placed on her. The stalls were small and she was glad to see him. Ben was paid to exercise the horses, but Zack suspected that he did very little for them. After tightening the cinch, Zack placed the bit in Betsy's mouth. She was not a very big horse, but she could really move when there was a need.

Betsy snorted awakening Ben.

"Howdy, Zack." He stood, blinked his eyes and pulled out his pocket watch. "How long you been here, boy?"

"Howdy, Ben. I ain't been here long."

"You fellers headin' home tonight? Here, let me help saddle up your pa's stallion. That big black is one more beautiful animal!"

"Yup," Zack replied. "Black Spirit really can move." Zack chose not to answer Ben's question. He checked the saddles on both horses and paid Ben for their care.

As Ben helped lead the animals across the dirt floor, he leaned close to Zack and almost whispered, "You all need to get on home, boy. I've been hearin' some mighty bad stuff about Big John. He ain't too happy that Mr. Bentley sorta' accused him of cheatin'. You know he's real bad news, son, and y'all really need to git on home!"

Zack tried to be calm, but the fear that had already been nagging at him rose in his throat. "Thanks, Ben, but Pa's already gone to Hawkeye's for another game tonight."

As Zack led the horses away, he heard Ben say, "Lord, have mercy on us tonight! Two of the meanest men in Florida is about t' tangle."

Chapter Three

Pa's Revenge

Zack led the horses to the back door of the tavern. Although everything was quiet, he suspected that just inside that wall, the tension was thick. Zack threw the reins over the hitching post and tied loose loops. He thought about waiting outside but after several nerve-wracking minutes, he changed his mind. The rusty hinges creaked eerily as he pushed the door open and stepped inside, leaving the door slightly ajar.

Kerosene lamps had been placed on wall shelves. Their glow created grotesque, slowly-moving patterns as a slight breeze from the door played on the thick smoke that filled the air. Five men sat at a wooden table, their cards held closely. Whiskey bottles, small glasses and ashtrays dotted each gambler's space, but Zack noticed that his pa's glass was untouched. Pa sat on the side of the table next to the back door.

No one acknowledged Zack's entrance. He sat on an old wooden bench along the wall close to the door. From there, he could see under the table. As was common, each man wore a gun. He noticed that Big John's holster was unsnapped and his gun lay loose, partially out of its holster.

Some of the players were already well on their way to inebriation. A couple of times Zack heard the slosh of whiskey as it poured into the glasses. His mouth began to salivate. He thought how comforting it would be if he could have just one drink right now to settle his nerves, but knew he had to keep a clear head. Swallowing several times, he forced himself to watch every move made around the table.

Once in a while someone would quietly say, "Hit me," or "Raise ya' " or "Call."

Each word stabbed Zack's heart with greater anxiety. Because each man wanted the other's full pay, he knew that it was just a matter of moments before something went wrong.

The zipping sound of shuffling cards continued as each man took his turn dealing.

Now it was Big John's turn to deal. Light from the lamps danced in his cold, black eyes. Between the sweltering June night and the strained intensity of the game, Big John's face was dripping with sweat.

Zack's sick feeling intensified and his heart began to beat faster as Big John shifted, ever so slightly to one side, removed his pistol from the holster and laid it across his knee.

He's gonna shoot Pa, for sure, Zack figured.

Zack glanced at each player as Big John began to skillfully manipulate the cards. John glared defiantly at William, holding his gaze a little longer than the others.

Pa won't flinch, Zack thought, as his pa sat, cold as steel with his arms loosely crossed at his belt, just below the table. A lump formed in Zack's throat when he saw his pa's left hand drop, unnoticed by the other players, to loosen his gun from the holster. As far as anyone else could tell, William had not moved a muscle, nor had his eyes left Big John's face.

Big John quickly began to deal the cards, but as he dealt the first one to William, William's right hand appeared, seemingly from nowhere. He forced both of Big John's huge hands to the table, pinning them there. Big John's right hand held a card that was still halfway under the deck in his left hand. Everyone could see that John was dealing William from the bottom of the deck.

Zack dared not breathe as he watched their gazes, locked in angry hatred. He saw the gun in William's left hand and knew what was coming next.

A shot rang out – then three more.

As Big John fell backward, his gun fell and scooted toward Zack. Zack's muscles quivered as his stiffened body momentarily pressed hard against the wall. He was unable to breathe. What could only have been three or four seconds, seemed like minutes. Everything in the room was quiet except for a strange gurgling sound coming from the floor where Big John lay convulsing. As far as Zack could tell, none of the other players had moved. Zack's nostrils flared as the smell of gunfire mixed with the tobacco smoke, whiskey, and body odor assaulted his senses. William had shot Big John, and then had taken out the three wall lamps. Fire quickly spread around one of the fragmented lights.

Coming to his senses, Zack, with one gigantic leap, flung open the here-to-fore slightly open door and landed between Betsy and Black Spirit. He jerked the reins from the hitching post and swung himself onto Betsy. Within moments, William rushed out and straddled Black Spirit.

The sound of flying hoofs was the only noise to be heard as they stirred up a huge cloud of dust behind them.

As they hurried past the stables, Zack saw Ben silhouetted in the stable door with a hand on each side of his head and heard him scream, "Oh, God, help!"

Zack figured that no one would follow them. Everyone was afraid of William Bentley. He also figured that Big John was dead because Pa was known as the best marksman in those parts, but he decided to ask anyway.

"You kill Big John, Pa?" Zack asked in a squeaky, but loud voice. His body was still quivering with terror.

William ignored the question and continued a hard gallop.

They ran another half-mile before William slowed. "I don't want the horses to get too tired before we get home," he explained.

"D'ja git your money back, Pa?"

" Everything on the table and Big John's money belt."

"How much ya' reckon?" Zack was worried about having enough to take care of the farm and the family.

"No way to know, boy!" William glanced at Zack. "Stop your sniveling! You're a man now. Act like it!"

Zack cleared his throat and took a deep breath. "How long do ya' think it'll take us ta' git home, Pa?"

William chuckled then said, "Zack, you ask too many questions!"

They hurried on in silence for about seven more miles. William pulled Black Spirit to a halt, and turned in the saddle, listening. He then dismounted and put his ear on the ground, making sure no horses were following.

Before riding on, he relit a half-smoked cigar. "Just around that next curve is a little dirt trail. We'll be turning left there."

"Why, Pa?" Zack was confused. "I thought we were going home."

William didn't answer, but with a gentle kick, he urged Black Spirit into a trot. Betsy followed and soon they were turning left on a narrow trail of powdery sand. Occasional weeds growing across the trail told Zack that it was seldom used. They rode about seventy-five feet and Pa pulled Black Spirit to a halt.

"Wait here," he whispered as he dismounted. Breaking a small bush, he again mounted and rode back to the main road, turning toward home.

Zack looked on in dismay. "Pa, where're ya goin?" he called in a coarse whisper.

With racing heart Zack glued his eyes on Pa as he turned Black Spirit onto a deer trail on the opposite side of the road. He knew not to move because Pa had said, "Wait here!"

Zack had waited about ten or fifteen minutes when he heard a noise behind him. Turning quickly, he saw Pa leading Black Spirit toward him.

Handing his reins to Zack he hurried to the road, a small, leafy bush in hand. Soon the tracks where they turned disappeared, leaving only the forward tracks on the main road, with one set of hoof prints turning right on the deer-trail. By the light of the moon,

Zack could see that there were no telltale tracks turning left for a posse to follow.

As much as Zack hated his father, he still recognized that Pa had an admirable, cunning knowledge of survival that few men possessed.

They quietly rode the seldom-used trail for almost an hour before seeing a few scattered pines. Coming to a small watery glade, Zack followed Pa's lead and dismounted.

As they walked a little farther, the road led into an old campsite. Long ago, several tall pines had been cut and scrub oaks were now making a stand. The fallen pines were still positioned around a depression in the sandy ground, indicating a long since abandoned fire hole. The outline of a thick stand of tall pine and oak trees loomed ahead. A solid cover of clouds had edged in and now shrouded the moon.

Zack followed Pa as he led the way into the eerie darkness.

"Pa, how do you know where we're going?" Zack asked. "I'm scared we're gonna' walk into sumthin'."

"Your eyes will get used to the dark soon. Just stay close to me."

William zigzagged through the stand of tall trees. On his right, Zack saw a dim light somewhere deep in the forest.

"It seems like we're headed right back where we started," Zack commented. "We're not lost are we, Pa?"

As was his way, William did not answer.

They made a sharp turn and were suddenly on a single file rabbit trail which they followed into a small clearing.

The best Zack could see, there was a dilapidated dwelling that was now overgrown with vines. The faint light glowing in a window must have been the light he had seen earlier. It looked to Zack like the house had long ago been a nice farmhouse.

William cupped his hands and whistled softly. The front door squeaked open just wide enough for a shotgun barrel to appear.

"Rose... Rosy! It's me – William."

The front door slowly opened and a disheveled head of long gray hair streaked with a few strands of black appeared. Zack stepped back in shock. *Could this wild, animal-looking creature really be a human?*

She stepped out, a shotgun in one hand and an oil lamp held high in the other. The light revealed a tattered mass of cloth that had probably been a dress at one time. The woman seemed so small that Zack wondered what held the rags in place.

"That really you, William?" she asked. Slightly turning her head from side to side she peered into the darkness. Her soft voice lightly trembled as she spoke. The light glimmering on her piercing eyes forced Zack back still another step.

"It's me, Rosy. I have Zack with me. Can we come in?"

"Who's Zack? I don't know no Zack. Y'all best just go. It's the middle of the night, boy."

"I know, Rosy, but I need to come in for a while."

Rose stepped back inside and leaned the shotgun against the door facing.

"I... I um... I'll stay out here with the horses, Pa. Who is this woman, anyhow?"

"She's my sister. She really is harmless." William allowed an understanding smile to play across his otherwise stern mouth. "I'll explain everything to you as soon as I get a chance."

Rose again appeared in the door. "If you'uns are commin', get on in here. Them infernal mosquitoes are fillin' the house."

Zack followed William into the dingy room then shut the door. He looked for a place to sit but found none. Every seat was piled high with *things*. There seemed to be only one large room and a kitchen, but on second glance, he noticed a room off to the left that he supposed to be a bedroom.

"Rose, this is my oldest son, Zack."

Rose made a half turn to look at Zack out of the corner of her eye. "Fine lookin' boy, William. How old is he?"

"He'll be eighteen this month," William answered.

"I ain't seen nobody since the last time you was here, William. It's good to see ya'." She moved several small piles of 'stuff' and revealed a deep-red, velvet love seat. The carving in the wood frame was fancier than Zack had ever seen.

"Sit here, son." Her voice was kind but guarded.

Zack sat on the love seat, letting his hand stroke the plush pile.

After she picked up some boxes, an overstuffed chair was revealed. "Here, William. Rest here while I get ya' some coffee."

"If you have some, I'd rather have whiskey, Rose," William told his sister.

Anger and fear flared her nostrils as she spoke through clenched teeth. "You know there won't ever be a drop of that devil's fire on *my* property, William Bentley."

Tears started down her cheeks as she quickly turned to go to the kitchen.

"Rosy, I'm sorry," he offered. "I forgot. Coffee will be just fine."

Zack had hardly moved a muscle. So much had happened since they left the paymaster's railcar. It seemed like days ago but he knew it had only been hours.

His mind whirled haphazardly from one thought to another. *What will happen to Pa? He'll have to be on the run from Sherriff Red. How can we make it with no money coming in? What is wrong with this pitiful woman that Pa is suddenly claiming as his sister? Why haven't I ever heard about her before?*

Rose brought a steaming cup of coffee to Zack. "Maybe this will help," she said. Her voice was soft and gentle, and her eyes had lost their sharp severity. "I've never met any of William's young'uns before. I'm real glad to know you, Zack."

The coffee was bitter but the warmth was soothing to his dusty throat.

"I— I'm glad to know you, too, Miss Rose."

"*Aunt* Rose," she corrected. "I'd be happy if you'd call me *Aunt* Rose."

Soon the coffee was gone and Zack's heavy eyes begin to blink. He wondered how long Pa would stay here. The drone of Aunt Rose and Pa quietly talking put him to sleep.

He had no idea how long he had slept, but the stress of impending danger for Pa and their family would not let him sleep soundly. Again he stirred and tuned into their conversation.

"Rosy," Pa hesitated slightly then continued. "I- I got myself in a little trouble again, and I'd really appreciate it if you don't tell anyone you saw me. Since Sheriff Red Cole knows you live here he may just come by here when he finds out I'm not home. He'll be looking for me, for sure."

Rose pushed a lock of unkempt hair off her face and glared at William.

"William Bentley!" Zack noticed her lips tighten as a terrible frown came over her thin, wrinkled face.

"I knew when you came here this hour of the night that you was in trouble again. What in *tarnation* have you done now?"

William pushed open the squeaky screen door and stepped onto the porch, followed by his agitated sister. As Zack pulled his weary body up to follow, he wondered if he could possibly make the rest of the ride home, but for sure Pa was leaving.

Leaning against the inside doorframe he flicked off some of the peeling paint with his fingernail, leaving a layer of dark green showing through the yellow. Pa and Aunt Rose sat on the steps as he told her that he had to get back his pay that Big John had stolen from him.

"How'd ja' get it back?" Rose's voice sounded accusing.

"I shot him, Rosy," William answered matter-of-factly.

"Heaven help you, William Bentley! I reckon you will spend the rest of your good-for-nothin' life runnin' or get yourself caught an' spend twenty more years in jail."

"Rosy, ju-"

"Don't *Rosy* me, William." She angrily shook a bony finger in his face. "If you had been home when you's supposed to be takin' care of Ruby and the children, you wouldn't be in this trouble." Suddenly her voice dropped from a high, loud frustrated pitch to a somber angry tone. "Just like if you'd been here when you was supposed to," she continued, "that wicked bunch of outlaws wouldn't have slaughtered my girls." Tears began to flow as Rose sat down on the step.

Zack was beginning to see a picture that he really didn't like. *I'll get Pa to tell me what happened*, Zack promised himself.

He opened the screen door as William put his big hand on Rose's shoulder. "I'm sorry, Rose." His voice was thoughtfully subdued as he then wrapped her tiny frame in his arms.

"We really do have to go. I have to get Zack home to take care of the homestead. No telling if I'll ever see you again, Rose, but..." The steps groaned pitifully as pa stood and hurried out to the horses. Zack imagined that they were both leaving behind a multitude of unspoken thoughts.

Zack stood beside his newly-found aunt, wondering what to say. He cleared his throat and whispered, "Aunt Rose, I would like to come back and help around here some day if you don't care. I'll have to take care of Ma and the young'uns now that Pa ain't gonna' be there no more, but I'll try to come back soon."

She lifted her tear-stained face then nodded without speaking.

Zack's mind raced with questions as he and William rode through the woods.

"Pa, what happened to Aunt Rose's family?"

William pulled Black Spirit to a halt and took a deep breath.

"I was head of an outlaw gang for several years before your ma and I were married, and for a couple of years after. I was supposed to meet my men at an abandoned shack that's about two-and-a-half-miles behind Rose's place." He took a long breath and explained that Rose's husband had died about a year before. He had been a logger and had received a nasty cut from a saw. Gangrene set in the wound, and six days later he was dead.

"There were some really bad men in my gang. They were all from South Georgia and knew nothing about this area or my family."

Zack thought that it sounded almost as though Pa was speaking to himself.

William took a moment to light his cigar before continuing. "I got tied up in a big game of poker and it lasted three days. I had no idea that the men would not wait for me where I told them to wait.

They were drinking and decided to rob the nearest place they found. That happened to be Rosy's home. They didn't know that she was my sister, and they told me it started out to be a simple robbery. Finding that there was no man around to stop them, they ended up

spending those three days raping Rose's three teenage girls, and then, when they were through with them, they killed them. They had already beat Rose and thought she was dead, but she survived. She has never been *right* since."

Zack felt sick. The little respect he had for his father now vanished, leaving a deathly sickening ache inside.

"What did you do about it, Pa?"

Pa continued, "I found four of them in the Everglades, and they've never been seen since. I heard that the other one went back to Georgia and started a new gang. I still expect to find him, if we both live long enough."

As William and Zack dismounted, Zack realized they were on a different trail than they had used coming into Aunt Rose's. Leading the horses, they walked another hundred or so yards and came to a small creek. William led Black Spirit into the water, walking upstream for about fifteen minutes.

Reaching another clearing, they left the creek-bed and again, straddled their horses. Twenty minutes later, they climbed a low hill. Just over the crest was a well-traveled road. Here their rides broke into a fast trot.

Suddenly, Zack realized they were almost home. He knew this area well, as he had traveled this road many times.

"Pa, how could we get here this fast? We musta' cut off at least a hour."

They slowed the horses to a walk before William answered.

"*An* hour, Zack," Pa corrected before continuing. "When I come back home, I expect you to be speaking better English. You have good study books at home. Use them and make something out of yourself that you can be proud of."

William took a deep breath and glanced behind them. "Ruby has been sending your brothers to school. I hope you will continue to make sure they each get a decent education since I won't be there to teach them."

William halted and looked at Zack. "Son, I'm not much of an example. I've never been the father you children need or the husband your mother needs. I want you to take control of the home place while I'm on the run..." his voice halted momentarily, "...or they might catch me. The law in these parts is pretty good. But if I go to prison, or whatever, I want you to learn to be a better man than I am."

Zack watched his father's face with mixed feelings, knowing he might never see him again.

William continued, "I'll leave most of this money with you and your ma, but I'll need some to keep me going." He pulled out the money-belt that he had taken off Big John and handed it to Zack. He then reached into his pocket and counted out enough to keep himself running for a while. The rest he handed to Zack.

"Do you understand what I'm telling you, Zack? You are going to have to be the one to help your mother raise the other children."

He started to ride on then decided to pause again to say, "You also need to know that Ruby will be birthing another child in a few months. See to it you get the doctor in plenty of time. She's getting older and will need experienced help." He seemed to ignore the fact that Zack was in shock.

"Can I depend on you, son?"

"Yes, Pa. I'll do what I can. I promise ya' – you."

Slapping Black's flank Pa said, "Let's ride. We're about two minutes from Ruby and the children."

After stopping to see that there were no strange horses around their place, and no horse tracks leading up to their house, Zack and Pa halted in the back yard.

Bubba, the big hound, ran out from under the house, his tail wagging his whole body. Bubba's sister, Baby, had been killed by a bear three years ago, but Zack still missed her excited glee when he would come home.

Zack took Betsy to the barn and unsaddled her, but he couldn't quell the feeling that he was having a horrible nightmare, and wished he could soon awaken.

As he walked back to the house, he heard Pa and Ma talking, and, as usual when Pa came home, his mother was crying.

Zack went into the kitchen just as Pa placed his arms around Ruby and kissed her. "They'll be here soon. Just be strong. Some day, Ruby, I'll make it all up to you, I promise."

Zack's hatred for Pa welled in him as William tore his mother's arms from his neck and hurried out the back door. She dropped to her knees, and her sobs told Zack that his anger was justified.

Zack turned to see William as he and Black Spirit hurried past, headed toward the swampy Everglades. The eastern sky was showing bright tints of beautiful color, silhouetting an ugly scene of a rider whom he hated, yet strangely admired.

"They'll never find him in them swamps, Ma," Zack reassured. As he helped his mother up to sit at the table, he noticed a fairly large bulge in her belly.

"Ma, I'm so sorry," he apologized, placing his arms around her.

"Son, it isn't your fault. Cain't *nobody* control William Bentley-*nobody!"* Her tears flowed unrestrained.

Remembering that it was Sunday, Zack said, "Ma, I ain't slept much since Friday night. I know its Sunday and you want to go to church. I hate to leave you here crying like this, but..."

"Go on to bed, Zack. We'll talk when you get up."

Gratefully, Zack turned toward the bedroom. Grasping a half-full bottle of whiskey as he walked by the homemade buffet, he realized it had not been touched since he left for the logging camp.

Chapter Four

Back Home

The aroma of home cooking aroused Zack from a deep sleep. His eyes seemed too heavy to open so he lay there, enjoying the comfort of a plush feather tick on a real bed.

Outside he heard J.J. and Harmony Bell playing hide-'n'-seek. Trying to sit, he realized the alcohol he'd drunk before going to bed still had his head swirling. Taking the bottle from the table he saw that there were only a couple more swallows. Downing them, he fell back on the bed.

The next time he opened his eyes the sun was high overhead. Bolting up, he wondered why it was so quiet. There were no laughing voices, no counting to one hundred, no sounds, and no smell of food cooking.

Pulling on his pants, Zack hurried to the living area. Finding no one there, he rushed through the breezeway past the kitchen to the back porch.

"Ma! – J.J.! - Harmony Bell! " His call sounded anxious. "Billy Jake!"

Before he finished his words, he heard his gleeful little sister, "Zack's awake!" She rushed from the barn with her arms outstretched. "Zack, I've missed you!"

Zack had missed her sweet embrace.

"Girl, you've really grown and gained some weight, too," he grunted as he lifted her.

"I'm Mama's big helper, now," she announced as J.J. and Ma came out of the barn.

J.J. set down a pail and ran to Zack. "Boy, it sure is good to have you home, Zack. I hope Pa ain't gonna' make you go back any time soon. It just ain't the same without you."

"I reckon I'll be staying home for a while, J.J. I missed all of you, too."

"There're some leftovers in the pie pantry, Zack. We've already had dinner. Go on and eat while we finish the chores. The cow just came in last week and she is giving a lot of milk."

Billy Jake came from the hog pen with the slop-pail in his hand.

"Hi, Zack," he yelled happily. "We've really missed you." He closed the gate and sauntered over to his big brother. "I'm hoping Suzie will be having babies in a couple more months. Mr. Watkins brought his boar over about three or four weeks ago and put him in the pen with Suzie for a week." Billy Jake spoke with pride. Suzie was a sow he had raised on a bottle. "Now she'll be birthin' in about two and a half months."

Zack went into the kitchen and opened the old pie safe. He ran his fingers over the decorative nail holes in the tin front.

I remember when Pa made this. He had just come home from prison, and this is the first thing I can remember him doing that brought Mama happiness.

He got a plate and started dipping mouth-watering creamed corn, field peas, and fresh sliced tomatoes. There were also baked sweet potatoes and some crispy fried chicken. On the bottom shelf was a beautiful blackberry cobbler. Zack placed it on the table within easy reach and sat down to eat.

As he took his first bite, he felt a tickle on his leg. Looking under the table he saw two huge brown eyes and the giggling face of Harmony Belle. She broke into a full laugh as Zack pulled her out and sat her on his knee. As she placed her chubby hands on his face, he remembered how comforting it was when he was gone, to think about his sweet little sister.

"Want to eat with me?" Zack asked cheerfully.

She nodded her head so hard that her long, light brown hair slapped Zack in the face.

"Good. Sit over there and I'll get you a plate."

Zack got a plate and went to the pie safe to dip her food.

"No, Zack. I want cobbler. Ma said we had to wait until you woke up and we could all eat cobbler together."

"I'm sorry. I didn't know."

"Where's Pa?" she asked innocently. "Why didn't he come home, too?"

Trying to think of the best answer, Zack welcomed the interruption when J.J. and Billy Jake came in from their chores.

"Great!" J.J. was eyeing the blackberry dessert. Billy Jake just smiled and pompously swaggered over to get a plate.

Ma leaned on the doorframe as she removed her shoes. "Get me one, too, Billy Jake," she requested. "My feet and back are killing me. I thought I would *never* get all the chores done."

"Zack," she continued, "you've been losin' weight. Have you been sick?"

"Don't reckon, Ma. I guess I've been missin' your cookin', that's all."

Zack finished his chicken and vegetables, then dipped a healthy serving of cobbler. Just as he put the first big bite in his mouth, the sound of hoof-beats in the front yard made him drop his fork. He jumped up and his chair fell to the floor with a loud clatter as he raced through the breezeway into the front room.

Four men were dismounting. Slowly they tied their horses to the porch rail and the Sheriff stepped onto the porch. Ruby opened the door to Sheriff Red Cole and the three men that Zack assumed made up a posse. Two of the men were normal height and build and, like Sheriff Cole, seemed rather good-natured. The fourth man was very tall, thin, and had a sour expression and a long, handlebar mustache. He had beady, pinpoint eyes and his neck seemed much too long. Zack immediately formed a distrust for him.

Harmony Belle was pulling on Zack's arm so he picked her up as he stepped past his mother onto the porch.

"What can I do for you, Sheriff Cole?" Ruby's voice was calm, but Zack knew her heart must be racing.

"I'm looking for William, Miss Ruby. Is he here?"

"Don't reckon he is, Sheriff. He's been loggin' with Osceola Company. He's been gone almost four months now."

Zack leaned against the wall as Harmony Belle laid her head on his shoulder. Ma was saying something about how she had no idea where he could be. Zack was trying to decide what would be the right thing to do.

"Zack, weren't you working with your pa?"

Zack was so consumed with his own thoughts that he didn't realize the Sheriff had spoken to him.

"Zack ... Zack" he spoke a little louder.

Zack put Harmony Belle down and stared at the sheriff while biting his upper lip with a frown of consternation.

"I ... I'm sorry sir. Were you talkin' to me?"

"I asked you, weren't you working with your father!"

"Yes, sir."

"Do you know where he is?"

"No, sir."

"Did you come home alone?"

"No, sir."

"Then you know what he did, don't you?"

Zack looked down and took a deep breath, trying to give himself time to figure how to answer.

"Billy Jake," Ruby said sternly, "take the children into the house and…better yet, take them to the back yard and play with them there."

"Ah, Ma! I want to hear what Pa did!"

"Do as I say, Billy Jake!" Her tone was final.

Zack welcomed the extra time to think, as Sheriff Red Cole had not moved his gaze from him.

He knows that I know that Pa killed Big John, and that I know which direction Pa headed, Zack thought. In his mind he could hear

Injun Billy Joe telling him that the truth always pays because God will stand by you when you are truthful. *God, I ain't much good, he prayed silently, but you know I'm tryin'.*

"I know what Pa did, Sheriff Red." He heard his mother gasp.

"All right, son, tell me about it."

"Come in and we'll talk." As Zack turned to lead the way into the house, he put his arm around his tearful mother and suddenly felt a calm within himself.

Zack noticed that the tall, thin man did not come in. Sheriff Red and one of the others sat on a homemade bench. Zack went to the kitchen to get more chairs and noticed the tall man speaking with Billy Jake and JJ. Ruby refused to sit when Zack offered her a chair, but stood behind Zack with her hands on his shoulders.

"Folks are saying that William shot Big John in cold blood. Is that true, boy?"

Zack cocked his head and answered slowly with a thoughtful frown. "Well, sir, I reckon I need to know what you mean by '*cold blood*'."

The heavy-set man with gray whiskers was beginning to show a little irritation. "Boy, that means he just shot him fur no reason! You know what he means."

"Well then, sir, he didn't shoot him in cold blood. He had a real good reason."

"What might that be, son?" Sheriff Red Cole had a reputation for having good self-control.

"Well, sir," Zack was trying to say the right thing, "Big John had been stealing from Pa, cheatin' you know. So Pa got tired of it and caught him red-handed. There weren't no doubt in *anybody's* mind that he was dealin' Pa from the bottom of the deck, 'cause Pa pinned both his hands to the table while he was dealin'. Everybody could see that he was pullin' Pa's from the bottom. I was there and saw it myself."

"Boy," Zack continued, in a strange type of admiration, "Big John could really handle them cards and, you know, put 'em right where he wanted 'em. That's why Pa shot him. Shore 'nuf! An' besides that, from the bench where I was sittin', I could see that Big John had already pulled his pistol from the holster and laid it across his knee. For sure he would have shot Pa if Pa hadn't got him first. "

"Then William brought you home?" the Sheriff continued. "Where did he go from here?"

"Red," the quiet deputy spoke, "I think we should search 'cause he might still be here." He stood up to look through the house. Zack was grateful for the interruption.

Zack felt Ruby's hand tighten on his shoulder. "Sheriff Cole, you got no right to search my home. We told you ain't nobody here 'cept me 'n the young'uns, and I ain't lyin' to ya'."

"Sorry, Miss Ruby. It's my job, you know."

While they were searching, Zack went to the back yard. JJ and Harmony Belle were sitting on the porch crying. Billy Jake was leaning against a post, whittling on a small stick.

"What happened, JJ?"

"That man sez he was goin' to catch our no-good Pa 'n hang him." He broke into violent sobs. "Don't let him hang Pa, Zack."

Zack jumped off the porch. "Where's he now?"

"He's in the barn."

Zack ran to the barn and asked, "What do you want out here?" His tone was angry and accusing.

"Boy, I know you're lying. You know where your Pa went, and we'll find him soon. When we do, he'll be hanged!"

Zack summoned all the strength he could and stood tall. "Mister, don't you ever again call me a liar, and don't you ever again tell my brothers and sister that you're gonna' hang their Pa. Simply weren't no call for that. Now get out of our barn."

The tall man glared at Zack and as he left, he muttered, "You young rascal. You're gonna' be just like your pa."

Zack watched the deputy walk toward the front yard and noticed that he displayed a definite limp.

When Zack went into the front yard, the sheriff had one foot in a stirrup. Zack stood in front of him and said, "Sheriff Cole, that man comin' from the back yard ain't never welcome at our house again. You'd be welcomed anytime, but he had better never show his face here again! Just ain't no tellin' what I might do!" His fiery tone and his demeanor were intense.

"All right, Zack, but wha'd he do?"

"He told the young'uns that he was gonna' hang their no good Pa, and he called me a liar. *Now* the young'uns are out there crying their hearts out. Sheriff Red, I was honest with you and didn't try to hide nothin'. Now you'd better keep that man away from my family."

"I'm sorry, son, and I do thank you for being so honest with me." He mounted his big red steed and promised, "As for the deputy, I'll handle it. Don't worry, Zack." He tipped his hat. "Good day, Miss Ruby."

After dark settled in, Ruby put the children to bed, and then found Zack sitting in the dark living room. Lighting a lamp, she sat down in her favorite rocker.

"Son, I know you feel like you are weighted down… like you have to be the one to run this place, and take care of me and the young'uns. I know I'll need a lot of help, but I don't want you to feel guilty for what your Pa's done. What he did was his own fault. You're a good boy, Zack, and I know you've had a hard life so far, but…"

"Ma," Zack interrupted. He paused, remembering that his father's last request was for Zack to take care of the family. "I promised Pa that I would take care of you and the young'uns and be responsible for seein' that things are kept up around here. I know… well, it weren't my fault that Pa killed Big John, but maybe…" he swallowed hard as tears began streaming down his cheeks, "…just maybe, if I hadn't been so afraid of him, I could have talked him into comin' on home. Then all this wouldn't have happened."

Ruby stood and hurried to the home-made sofa and sat beside her son.

"Zack, it's all gonna be all right. I know you'll do all you can and I'll do all I can, and we'll just have to leave the rest to God. Do you remember not long before you went loggin' with William you was reading the Bible to me one evening?"

Zack nodded.

"Remember, you read where Jesus said, *I will never leave you or forsake you*, and another place Jesus said for us to cast our cares on Him?"

Zack wiped his tears on his sleeve and nodded again.

"Son, that's what we've got to do. I really learned to depend on Christ while you and your pa was gone this time, and He ain't failed me yet!"

"But, Ma, you are good enough that He'll hear you. I'm such a bad person that… well, how can I know He'll even listen to me, let alone help me?"

"He *does* hear you, and He *will* help you."

Ruby put her arms around Zack. He laid his head on her shoulder and enjoyed the warmth and strength of her tender, motherly love.

Chapter Five

Zack Remembers

Zack closed the squeaking door behind him. He had gone to bed but, unable to sleep, he decided to go outside to sit on the front steps. The breeze was gentle for a mid-June night.

He took a deep breath and knew that rain was on the way.

It was good to be home, but now the responsibility of running the homestead was almost more than he could handle.

I absolutely must stop drinking, he thought. *What if something happened to Ma or one of the young'uns and I was drunk. I couldn't do anything to help.*

He sat on the porch and drew his long legs up the steps, propelling his knobby knees almost to his armpit. There with his head in the crook of his arm, he began mulling over his fear, and anger, and growing hatred for his father.

Even if he was mean to Ma and the young'uns, he thought, *at least he knew what to do if something happened. Now I have to...*

Zack looked up at the trees as they blew and noticed that the gentle breeze was becoming a little stronger.

"Please, God," he spoke aloud as tears began to flow. "I can't do this alone. God, I know I ain't supposed to hate anybody, but you know how mean Pa is and how he has always made Ma and me the young'uns cry. When he was drinkin', he would beat all of us–even

Ma, and he would break stuff, good stuff, that Ma or the young'uns wanted real bad, and then he'd make me try to fix it."

He stopped praying as he remembered some of the terrible beatings William had given him and the two younger boys—that, after Pa fell unconscious in a drunken stupor, he would sneak into his brother's room and put salve on their wounds as well as his own. He remembered holding them to still their trembling bodies, even though his own anguish may have been just as severe. He was well aware of the terrible pain they suffered.

Ma would have done it, he reasoned, *but she was not allowed to.*

He thought for a second, and then silently continued his prayer.

God, I know I ain't supposed to, but I hate Pa. Don't git me wrong, now, 'cause, in some strange way I reckon I love him, too, but...but... why couldn't he be good and kind like Ma an' the young'uns deserve?

Tears were now freely flowing down his cheeks, and he didn't notice that a few scattered raindrops were also falling.

Sitting on the steps he began to remember the first time he ever realized he had a father. The memories began to play through his mind with vivid accuracy. In a torrent of tears, he buried his face in the bend of his arm, and remembered.

"Get up, Zack." Ma was shaking him. "Hurry and get dressed. We're goin' for a ride."

Zack sat up and rubbed his eyes. "Ma, it's dark outside. Where're we goin'?"

"Hurry up, now. I want you to help me load the wagon. There's a basket of food on the table and the wagon's out front. I have to get Billy Jake dressed."

Zack dressed and sat on the side of the bed yawning.

Ma hurried past his door carrying two-year-old Billy Jake, wrapped in a blanket. "Come on, Zack. We have to hurry."

Zack got dressed, then shuffled his sleepy, yawning self into the kitchen and hefted a huge basket of food into his arms. It was heavy, but he carried it to the front porch where Ma took it and loaded it in the wagon.

"Climb in, Zack, while I get the rest of the stuff."

Ma had made a pallet in the wagon bed and Billy Jake was sleeping soundly. Zack crawled under the warm quilt that his mother and Aunt Rita made and wondered where Ma was taking them. She had never done anything like this before. He heard the front door shut and Ma's shoes clicking down the steps. She climbed onto the seat and took the reins.

As the wagon began to bump over the rough yard, Zack sat up and again asked, "Ma, where we goin'?"

"It will be a long ride, Zack, so just lie down and sleep."

Again he snuggled under the cozy quilt and was soon asleep.

When Zack awakened, the horses were still clip-clopping along. He raised himself on his elbows and stretched his neck, trying to look over the sideboard, but he didn't recognize anything. The wagon rumbled across a little wooden bridge from where he saw a few people scattered along the creek banks with cane poles in their hands. The sun sparkled on the clear water as it rippled toward the bridge.

Suddenly there was a shrill whistle and a frightening hiss that caused him to bolt straight up. He threw the quilt off of himself and Billy Jake, and then scrambled onto the seat by Ma without saying a word.

Ma began to laugh at him and patted his trembling leg. "It's all right, Zack."

Zack noticed a railroad was running close beside the road, and a huge black locomotive with a bright red cow-catcher was coming toward them. Steam spewed from each side, blowing so hard that the tall grass was lying almost flat, fluttering in waves like the water he had seen on the Okeechobee. Smoke erupted from a smoke stack, billowing clouds of black puffs high into the air. The earsplitting sound of escaping steam, the piercing blast of its whistle, and the noise of steel wheels grating on the metal tracks as the long train was slowing, had severely unnerved Zack.

"Is that a train, Ma?" asked Zack. "Aunt Rita told me about riding on one, and that looks just like she said."

"That's a train, Zack."

Zack sat quietly watching the amazing contraption until they were well past it. He wondered how Billy Jake could sleep through all that commotion.

Where are we goin', Ma? We ain't never gone this far before, have we, Ma?"

"We're going to see William, son. He's your pa."

"My pa!" Zack exclaimed. "I ain't got no pa." Zack spoke in angry confusion. He had heard Ma and Aunt Rita and others talking about William, but he never realized that William was his daddy.

"Everybody has a father, Zack, and William is yours."

Billy Jake began to cry, so Zack climbed to the back and lifted his little brother to the seat between himself and Ma.

"I hung'y, Ma." His little voice was tearful.

"We'll stop in a little while–not more than an hour or so. Then you can eat."

Billy Jake's bottom lip protruded as he laid his head on Zack's shoulder.

"How come I never get to see my pa?" Zack was troubled by the situation. *Other children I know have their pa's living in the house with them,* he thought.

"He can't come home just yet."

Mother used her whip to make the horses trot faster.

They began to see houses, which had been built close together. There were also a number of wagons as well as an occasional horse-drawn buggy. Zack soon forgot that he had a pa as he eagerly absorbed many sights and sounds of a town.

He began to notice large, strange buildings, so close that some of them, he thought, had grown together.

"This is Moore Haven," Ruby announced. "Your pa is just a little ways the other side of town."

Everything was bright and colorful and people were in and out of the stores. Zack wondered what they were doing.

There were many things here that he had never seen before but the strangest thing he had ever seen was a funny looking buggy that wasn't even pulled by a horse. It was moving all by itself.

"Ma," shouted Zack as he pointed to the strange black and brown contraption. "Look, look! What's that thing?"

"That's a Model 'T'. I reckon this is the first one you've ever seen. I ain't seen many of them. Rich folks have them. Reckon there ain't no rich folks around where we live."

"There ain't no horse! How does it move, Ma?"

"There's an engine in it. I don't understand much about it, but I know you have to buy fuel for it at the pharmacy."

Before long they were crossing a bridge. Looking down into the water, Zack became fearful.

"Ma," he cried as he tightened his grip on little Billy Jake. "Don't get too close to the edge! What if we fall off? Me an' Billy Jake can't swim."

Mother giggled. "It's all right, Zack. I've driven this rig over this bridge several times. This is the Caloosahatchee canal."

"What?" questioned Zack. "Cal-clu-cha-cha-chee?"

Mother broke into a loud, happy laugh, so Zack and Billy Jake joined in.

A short distance beyond the main town, Ma turned onto a narrow road. She pointed to a large red brick building with a very high wire fence around it.

"That's where we'll see your father, Zack."

They rode up to a big gate. In a moment a man who was holding a long gun opened it, and Ruby drove the wagon through. The gate was then closed behind them and the big lock put back.

They stopped just inside the gate and the man told Ma to get out. He looked all through the wagon, under the quilts, and around the front seat, then helped Ma back up. "Looks like a real good dinner, Miss Bentley. Have a good day."

Driving the wagon to a large grassy area, Ruby stopped and got down. She unhitched the horses and tethered them to a pole under a shade tree.

"Zack," she said, "hand me that folded quilt behind your seat." She spread it on a beautiful spot of shady grass. Going back to the wagon she lifted Billy Jake down to play.

"Do you want to help me with the food, Zack?"

Just as they got the basket of food down, a tall, thin man with a very long mustache and a long gun walked toward them. He had a noticeable limp in his left leg.

"Can I help you, Ma'am?"

"We're here for a visit with William Bentley," Ruby answered.

The man's jaw tightened as his left eyebrow raised sharply. A resulting frown accompanied the disapproving grunt that came from his extra long, lumpy throat. Cupping his hands around his mouth, he called to a man who stood at the door to the big building. "William Bentley," he barked. Without another word he turned back to stare at them while twirling one side of his extraordinarily long mustache in his fingers.

Zack noticed three other men walking around the yard and they each had long guns and they were all dressed the same as the skinny man standing close to him.

Soon another man came out of the big house. He looked different, as he had on blue clothes with wide white stripes.

As they got closer, Zack noticed that the man in stripes started walking faster and had a big smile on his face. He was rather tall and had a handsome face, but Zack didn't like the way he looked at Ma.

"Two hours, William, and I'll be back." The skinny, mean-looking man made the announcement as he turned back to the big, red brick house.

The other men with guns all left and William hugged and kissed Ruby for a long time. She began to cry, and that made Zack furious.

He then came to Zack, and before he knew what was happening, William had picked him up and hugged and kissed him, too. When he turned to pick up Billy Jake, Zack wiped his face so hard it began to sting.

Ma put her hand on each boy's shoulder and said, "Boys, this is your pa."

William smiled at the boys. Zack was afraid he was going to kiss him again, so he stepped behind his little brother.

"The boys are hungry, William. I'm going to let them eat." Ruby had stopped crying and was setting the food out on one of the quilts. She unpacked the food and placed plates, cups, and forks around the quilt. There was ham, corn-on-the-cob, mashed potatoes and gravy, garden peas, sliced tomatoes and cornbread, but best of all, she had made a mouth-watering chocolate cake. Zack wondered why this stranger should have such a special treat.

"This is great! I haven't had good food since I left home. The food here is just barely decent enough to keep a man alive."

Although he would have liked to refuse to eat with this unwanted, newly found *pa*, Zack's hunger pangs quickly had their way and he began to eat.

Later, Billy Jake went to sleep on a pallet that Ma made in the shade of the big banyan tree, but Zack had no intentions of sleeping.

No telling what this man might do, he thought.

He backed a few feet away from the adults. He then sat on the ground under the huge banyan and leaned against one of the many long support roots that grew straight down in the middle of the mammoth branches.

Carefully studying Pa's face, Zack decided that he was nice looking, but there was something about him that could not be trusted. Ruby and William sat close together and held hands, talking secretly.

Finally, Zack noticed the mustache man coming toward them so he got up and stood beside Ruby.

"Time's up, Bentley," the guard snapped. Again that skinny man looked fiercely angry as he glared at William and Ma. Frightened, Zack stepped behind Ruby's long, full skirt.

William lifted Zack and hugged him tightly as he kissed his cheek again. "Take good care of your Ma until I get home, son."

As soon as he could, he again wiped the kiss from his face and mumbled under his breath, "I ain't your son."

After holding Billy Jake and playfully rubbing his knuckles through his hair, William placed him on the wagon seat beside Zack and then wrapped his arms around Ruby. He hugged and kissed her until her face and neck turned real red, then lifted her onto the wagon seat. Zack decided right then that he would never like William, even if he was his pa.

"I'm sorry things have been so hard on you, Ruby. I won't have to stay here much longer."

Ruby handed William a big cloth in which she had tied up all the leftover food. He then turned toward the big building and never looked back. Zack watched with many emotions as his newly found pa entered the big house.

The man with the long mustache didn't move. He stood there glaring at them for a few seconds, his beady, mean eyes forced Zack to look the other way. When he looked back, the mean man with a very long gun was limping back to the building.

In another minute, Ma was driving the horses through the Iron Gate, and soon they were on their way back home.

Zack sat in silence with Billy Jake between himself and his mother. He noticed that Ma was crying. Zack clenched his teeth, pulled his eyebrows together and puckered his lips into tight wrinkles. He was convinced that he hated William Bentley. *Why did he have to go and make Ma cry?*

As soon as they crossed the Caloosahatchee canal, and rode through Moore Haven, Billy Jake and Zack curled up on the soft quilts in the wagon bed. Soon his baby brother was asleep, but Zack was not sleepy. He wondered if it might be nice to have a pa living at home. Would he do all the things around the house that their neighbors and Injun Billy Joe did now? Ma acted like she was real proud to see Pa, even if she did cry.

Finally sleep overtook him.

When Zack awoke, he climbed onto the seat beside Ma.

"Well, Zack, what do you think of your pa?"

“”I don’t like him a bit, Ma,” he said stubbornly. “He makes you cry an’ I don’t like him to kiss me.”

Ruby smiled. “He will probably be home in about five or six more months. I’m sure you’ll get used to him.”

Zack crossed his arms in defiance. “He ain’t my pa,” he said under his breath. “I don’t have a pa.”

“William is your pa, Zack. You’ll get used to him,” she repeated.

It was almost dark when they pulled the wagon to a halt in front of Aunt Rita’s house. They lived about a half-mile outside of Clewiston. Zack’s cousins came running to greet them as Aunt Rita stepped onto the porch.

“Y’all come on in,” she hollered. “I got supper almost ready.”

Ruby lifted Billy Jake from the wagon and went in with Aunt Rita.

“Come on, Zack. Let’s play. Pa made us a big swing. It goes really high.”

“It’s gettin’ dark a’ready,” Zack objected, but walked to the side yard where a very long rope was attached to a limb and a small wooden plank made a seat. Zack knew that Ma and Aunt Rita would be discussing their trip and he wanted to hear what they said.

“I don’t feel like playing, Bobby. I’m real tired.” He hated to see disappointment spread over his cousin’s face but he went inside anyway.

The women were already talking. Unnoticed, Zack sat on the floor beside the door.

“How much longer has William got?” Rita questioned.

“I think he’ll be home in about six more months, Rita. I know we need him, but sometimes I get afraid for him to come back. I don’t know how I really do feel.”

“I know, Ruby. If he would just stop drinkin’ that rot-gut whiskey, he could be a pretty good man. What did they put him in prison for this time anyway? I don’t think I ever did know the whole story.”

“Well, he stole all that stuff from Green’s mercantile, and also was makin’ moonshine and selling it. Then there was that old robbery charge that they finally pinned on him... you remember; the one when he was playin' poker and took off with most of the money. I guess all that added up to about three years."

"Oh, Ruby, I do wish he would settle down and quit drinkin' an' gamblin' and take care of his family!"

"He promised me that he would never drink again, but I doubt that he will really quit. He stops for a couple of months, but in a little while he starts again. That's when he gets mean and beats the kids and me. That's also when he starts makin' an' sellin' moonshine so he'll have money to pay for what he gambles an' drinks."

Zack was learning why his father was in prison. He made and drank whiskey and stole things.

Right then he told himself he would never, as long as he lived, drink whiskey or steal anything. *I'll never be like Pa,* he promised himself.

Now, here I am, Zack reasoned, *and I drink as bad as Pa does.*

Suddenly Zack realized a torrential rain was drenching him. The storm had blown in and lightening was flashing all around. Thunder reverberated through the sky, and as he looked up, a bolt of lightening hit a tall pine. It split it from top to bottom and ran about twenty feet along the ground. Part of the tree fell into the yard, missing the house by less than ten feet. Limbs were breaking and blowing across the yard, but Zack didn't move.

I wouldn't care if I did get lightnin' struck, he thought. *At least I wouldn't end up killin' somebody like Pa did.*

He put his head back down in the crook of his arm.

This wind will probably blow more of the roof off the old barn, he thought, *and it ain't even been repaired yet from the hurricane last year.*

Zack felt his mother's hands on his shoulders. Just then a bright flash lit the yard as though it was day. "My Goodness, son," she said with trepidation. "There's a tree down in the yard!

"Zack," she admonished, "you can't stay out here like this. You will catch your death of cold, and you might even get hit by lightning."

As he stood to go inside, he said, "Would it matter if I did, Ma? I doubt if anybody would care."

"Oh, Zack!" She shut and bolted the door then wrapped a towel around his shivering body. "Don't be silly. You know we would care very much."

They sat on the wooden seat that Pa had made for a sofa. She wrapped her arms around him as she pulled his soggy head onto her shoulder. "You are very much loved and needed, Zack."

He felt like that five-year-old boy that he was remembering just a few minutes ago.

"I just don't know how I could ever make it if you weren't here to help me. I'm going to have a baby before long, and I'll need you to be here for me and the kids."

Zack wiped his face and curly black hair on the towel, straightened himself and took his mother's hands.

"I know, Ma, and I'll be here for you, an' I promise I'll stop drinkin'. I don't ever want to turn out like Pa."

Since Ruby didn't answer, Zack figured she was probably remembering William's voice saying those exact words.

"Ma," Zack said thoughtfully, "You know that tall, thin man that came with Sheriff Cole today?"

Ruby nodded.

"Well, I know now where I knowed--knew him from. Do you remember the first time you took me to the prison to see Pa?"

Ruby looked at him with a surprised frown as she tried to remember.

Zack continued. "Well, that is where I first saw him. He was that mean, skinny man with the long handlebar mustache that brought Pa out to eat dinner with us. I didn't like him then, an' I don't like him now. He knew us, too, Ma. I bet he's mad at Pa about something an' wants to find him just to kill him."

"Zack, how can you remem... You know, I think that *was* the same man." She thought a moment then continued. "I wonder if that could be the guard that William told me about that he had trouble with in prison? I think he said they got into a fight over something about a gamblin' game and William beat him up before the other guards could get to them. My goodness!" she exclaimed. "He also told me that he had broken the guard's leg in the brawl. I think you're right, Zack, but you were so young. How can you remember that?"

"Ma, I sat out there in the rain awhile ago and remembered every detail about that trip. I felt so bad 'cause I hate Pa for leaving us all the time, and I realized I have always hated him, ever since I first found out I have a pa."

Ruby tightened her grip around his wet shoulders. "I'm sorry, Zack. When I first met William he was so much fun. He'd take me to the dance hall and we'd dance and laugh into the wee hours of the morning."

Her voice trailed away and Zack realized she was reliving a time when they were very much in love.

"Ma, I'm sure that somewhere in Pa there is some good, but I don't see it very often. He has never been here for you or me or the young'uns, and now there is another one on the way. I reckon he won't be here for this one either, will he Ma?"

Ruby placed her hand on her stomach and a little smile played over her face.

Zack continued. "I know I ain't much good, Ma, but I will try to do better. I'll be here for you. When d'ya reckon the birthin' will be?"

"I figure it'll be sometime in late October, or early November."

Zack had begun to shiver.

"Boy, get in there an' get on some dry clothes an' go to bed. It's already after twelve o'clock and we have a lot of chores come daybreak."

As Zack stood he noticed how pale and fragile his mother looked. He bent over and kissed her forehead. "I'll be up ta' help you, Ma."

Chapter Six

Injun Billy Joe

The next morning Zack awakened to the smell of frying bacon and sat on the edge of the bed. He ached all over but knew he had to get up and do chores and see if last night's storm had damaged the barn. The younger children were still asleep. In the kitchen, his mother sang as she worked.

"Good morning, Zack. It'll be ready in about twenty minutes."

"Mornin' Ma. I'm gonna' run out an' check the barn. I figure that wind last night might'a done some damage."

He stepped onto the porch. Light was just breaking in the east. It appeared to be about the same time as the morning Pa came bounding around the corner, riding Black Spirit past him as he headed for the 'Glades.

Zack hurried to the barn. All he had on his mind was finding the bottle that he had stashed. He was beginning to shake and knew that only his booze could steady his shaking hands.

Bubba strolled out of the woods to greet him. Zack stopped, about five feet from the barn and stooped to pet Bubba before going in.

Opening the barn door, he stepped inside and headed straight for his hiding place. His bottle wasn't there! Fretfully he started searching everywhere he might have left it. It was not to be found. He sat down on a hay bale and ran a shaking hand over dry lips.

"Looking for liquid fire?" Injun Billy Joe's voice was knowing, but not accusing.

Zack froze. In a corner stood Injun Billy Joe, holding a bottle of whiskey.

"Hey," Zack smiled as he greeted his friend. "I've really missed you." Then he questioned, "What are you doing here this time of the morning?" Before he could answer, Zack continued, "How d'ja know what I was looking for?"

"The way you are shaking, it is not hard to know." He sat on the little milking stool and continued. "Zack, I know what happened with Mister William. Now you will have a very heavy responsibility and you cannot function unless you control yourself."

Billy Joe had learned proper English in the missionary's school. It sounded almost foreign to Zack.

"I *am* going to, but right now I really need a drink... just enough t' git me through the day."

"Do you remember what I have told you so many times, and what you have heard in the sermons preached by Parson Smith—that you can't do it without God's help? If you will let me, I will pray now and you *will* make it through the day."

Subdued, Zack submitted.

Billy Joe prayed a very simple but sincere prayer.

"Thank you, Billy Joe. I will try to make it today." Zack noticed his hands were not shaking as badly.

"I've come here at least once a week since you have been gone. I want to make sure the animals are taken care of. Since your mother is with child, she depends on Billy Jake to do most of the chores, and that is very hard for him. I come in before he awakens and do some of the heavy work."

"Nobody could ever ask for a better friend," Zack said. "Do you reckon Ma will be all right?"

"Your mother has been very tired lately. She needs some of the fresh herbs from the swamp. I will bring them to you tomorrow and tell you how to prepare a tea for her. They will make her feel much better."

"Pa said she is getting older and she might have trouble. What do you think, Billy Joe?"

"Miss Ruby needs rest and good food. I think she will do fine if she will take the herbs I bring. You make sure she drinks her tea every day." He paused, then said, "I imagine the child will be born by the middle of October."

"Really?" Zack questioned. "Ma said it will probably be sometime in late October or early November."

"The moon tells a lot, but with your mother's health as it is, I don't believe she will be able to go to full term."

"Well, I'll make sure she takes her tea. I just hope I'll know what to do when the time comes, Billy Joe."

Zack picked up a hay-fork and pitched some feed to the cow. "Billy Joe," he said, "I need to check the barn to see if any more damage was done last night. We haven't even had the money to repair the damage done by the hurricane last year."

"I've already looked, Zack. There is a little more damage, but I will help you repair it. Do you have enough money to buy the supplies you need?"

"I think I have enough to do all the repairs–last years and this new damage. I hid all our money where it'll be safe. It's got to last until I can get a job.

"Zack," mother called. "Come to breakfast 'fore it gets cold."

Zack and Billy Joe stepped from the barn.

"Good morning, Miss Ruby," Billy Joe said cheerfully.

"Well, Billy Joe!" mother exclaimed. "I had no idea you was here. Come on in and have breakfast with us. I have plenty cooked."

Knowing Billy Joe's habits, Zack figured he would gracefully refuse as he had done many times over the years.

"Thank you Miss Ruby. I would like to eat with you this morning as there are some things I want to talk to you and Zack about."

As they neared the house, Zack could hear the children playing around in the kitchen.

"Howdy, Billy Joe," Billy Jake said with a broad smile.

"Hello, Billy Jake. How have you been doing?"

Before he could answer, Harmony Belle ran from the bedroom, shoes and socks in hand. "Mister Billy Joe!" her sweet baby voice sang in excitement. She stood in front of him holding up her shoes and socks and tilted her head with a captivating smile of expectation. Light brown curls fell across her big brown eyes.

"You would like for me to help, little one?" he inquired.

She nodded vigorously. He placed her in a chair and prepared her small, chubby feet for a day of playing.

The table was set with food from their own farm.

A large chunk of fresh-churned butter and a jar of tangy, sweet guava jelly were waiting to melt on hot, flaky biscuits that Ruby had piled in a breadbasket. Big bowls of white-flour gravy, bacon, and scrambled eggs finished the tongue-tingling breakfast.

After offering a prayer of thanksgiving, an uncommon silence settled over everyone, as their mouths were too full for conversation.

"JJ," Ruby said, when they were finished eating, "you and Billy Jake hurry on out to do your chores and take Harmony Belle with you."

"Aw, Ma," Billy Jake said, "I want to stay in here and listen to Injun Billy Joe."

"Now, Billy Jake," Ruby said in a quiet but stern tone.

"Yes, Ma," Billy Jake answered obediently.

As the children were leaving, Ruby poured a second cup of coffee for Billy Joe, Zack, and herself.

"A couple of boards blowed... I mean blew off the barn last night, Ma. I'm just glad the lightening didn't set it on fire. It shouldn't be too hard to fix."

"I'm sure you'll handle it just fine, Son. I guess it needs to be done before more rain comes. I'd hate for the hay ta' git wet again. What did you want t' talk to us about, Billy Joe?"

Their Indian friend cleared his throat. "Miss Ruby, I'm very sorry about what Mister William did. It will surely make it very hard on all of you."

Ruby took a deep breath. "Thank you, Billy Joe. I know it'll be hard all right, but ain't that the way it's always been?" Her question seemed to serve as a resignation to fate.

"You must keep faith, Miss Ruby. God will be with you, and so will I."

Her faint smile and nod to her dear friend who had been so faithful to her family since they had moved to the homestead was sufficient thanks.

"There are a couple of things I want to discuss with you," Billy Joe continued.

Zack turned his chair to more directly face Injun Billy Joe.

"Zack, how many guns do you have?"

The query took Zack by surprise. He thoughtfully ran his fingers through his curly black hair as though that would help him think.

"Well," he began slowly, "I have my hunting rifle, and Pa left a rifle and a shotgun here, and I think his old thirty-eight pistol is in his room, ain't it, Ma?"

"That's right, Son, and I also have a shotgun that your pa gave me right after we married."

"How much ammunition have you?" Injun Billy Joe asked.

"I don't reckon there's any for Pa's rifle, and I don't think there's much for the shotgun. Why do ya' ask?"

"There's a gang of outlaws that have been working the Orlando area. They seem to be outsmarting the law, with every crime they commit. They are working their way south."

"I don't see how that is going to affect us, Billy." Ruby shrugged off the situation. "My guess would be that they'd head on past us to Miami and the Keys. There are a lot of places down there for them to hide out and lots of rich people to steal from."

Zack thought there must be a reason for Injun Billy Joe's concern.

"What's your point, Billy Joe?"

"Rumor has it that the gang boss has been asking questions about William Bentley, trying to locate him."

Zack noticed his mother stiffen with a slight gasp.

"I wonder if that could be the one gang member that Pa wasn't able to find, when his gang ravaged Aunt Rose's home place?"

"Zack!" Ruby exclaimed. "What do... who... How do you know about... I'm sure she died long ago!" Ruby was flabbergasted.

Zack studied her face in silence. *Did she not know that Aunt Rose still lived at the same homeplace?*

Billy Joe continued. "I think you would do well to go into town today and get fresh ammunition for all your weapons."

"Also, there is one more reason to get plenty of protection. A very big rouge black bear has been getting the farmer's livestock again."

Zack frowned and, with both hands planted firmly on the table, stood and leaned across the table toward Injun Billy Joe.

"We'll go get him!" he declared with determination.

"Zack!" Ruby admonished. "You are too young for that kind of hunt."

"We can't go get him yet, Zack." Billy Joe ignored Ruby's statement. "So far he has left no good trail for us to follow. One day soon he will make a mistake and then we will get him."

Zack walked to the water bucket and took the dipper off the twenty-penny nail that he had watched Pa pound into the rough-sawed kitchen timber the first time he came home from prison. In deep thought, he ran his fingers over the three-gallon bucket made of cedar staves, bound together with brass hoops. The tin dipper made the cool well water seem even colder. He quickly downed a dipper full then walked outside. Leaning a shoulder against one of the porch posts that supported the tin roof, he rolled his last cigarette and crushed the empty package.

Dishes rattled in the kitchen as Ruby nervously cleared the table.

Had the rusty-hinged screen-door not tattled, Zack would not have known that Billy Joe had stepped onto the porch. He placed a caring hand on Zack's shoulder.

"I know your responsibilities are heavy, my friend. I also see your hands are shaking badly, but the bottle will not help you. You must be strong, as your family needs you more now than ever."

"Injun Joe, why do you think that outlaw's askin' for Pa?"

"I'm not sure, Zack, but it has been told that he killed all the members of his old gang except one. I also heard that that one went to Georgia. It would make sense that he is the same man. I figure he has put another gang together."

They stood in silence for a moment, then Billy Joe continued.

"Did your father tell you about Miss Rose?"

"I never knowed she existed 'til Pa took me by her place after he shot Big John."

Billy Joe nodded. "It has been several years since I saw your aunt, but she was in bad condition. I really thought she might be dead by now."

"You think she'll be in any danger, Billy Joe? If that's the same man, he sure knows where she lives."

"I suppose so, but you need to concentrate on keeping your mother and the children safe for now."

As Billy Joe stepped into the yard he said, "Io has been asking about you lately. She is in town today, selling her hand-made baskets in front of the Mercantile. I'm sure she will be happy to see you."

Zack felt a strange flutter in his chest as he thought about Billy Joe's niece.

"Thanks, Billy Joe. I'll see her when I go to town for ammunition and supplies." Though he tried to sound nonchalant, a silly squeak in his voice announced his, otherwise hidden excitement.

Billy Joe flashed a knowing smile. "Try not to worry about anything, Zack. You must learn to trust God. Also, I'll be here to help when I can, but for the next few days I will be busy with repairs to *my* home. The storm damaged it quite badly last night."

"I'll come help ya' fix it, Billy Joe."

"It is not that bad, Zack. You go take care of your business in town. That is much more important right now. Goodbye, Zack, and say 'hello' to Io for me."

Zack watched his friend until he disappeared into the nearby woods.

I wish I could be good like Injun Billy Joe, he thought with conviction.

Chapter Seven

Jo

Zack went into his room and shoved his bed over a couple of feet. Then he carefully lifted one of the loose planks from the floor, exposing his secret hiding place.

As a child, he made a wooden box and nailed it securely to the floor joist.

Through the years he had placed many treasures in it, like his prettiest rocks, coins, small toys, or Indian arrow heads, most of which were still there. Once it was the burial place for his favorite frog when it died.

Now it served as a safe for the money Pa left with him to keep the family going.

Taking enough bills to cover repairs, ammunition, and food, he poked it into his shirt pocket.

After replacing the plank, he pulled his bed back in place.

In the kitchen, Ruby was leaning against the wall, seemingly in deep thought.

"You all right, Ma?"

Startled, she turned and smiled faintly. "I'm fine, Zack. I was just thinking about what Injun Billy Joe said." Pulling a chair away from the table, she sat down. "Are you about ready to go?"

"Soon as I hitch Betsy to the wagon," he said. "Is there anything special you need, Ma?"

"Just the usual, I reckon. Get another sack of flour, a peck of corn meal, a large bag of grain coffee, a gallon of cane syrup, and a big box of oatmeal. Oh, yes, we need sugar, too."

"I'll try not to be too late, Ma. Make sure the boys stay close to the house. They can help if you need something."

"Quit worrying 'bout us, boy. We made it just fine while you was off loggin' with your pa," she chided with a loving smile. "By the way, we're almost out of salt, and I'd also like to have three big boxes of corn flakes. Pretty soon I won't feel like cooking, and that will be a good fast breakfast for you young'uns."

Zack looked at the coffee grinder that was mounted on the wall and said, "Ma, I thought the grinder was broken. How are you goin' to grind that coffee after its parched?"

"I fixed it last week. It works just fine."

Realizing he had to buy more groceries than usual, Zack went back to his room and pulled more money from his secret box.

"I'll be back before dark, Ma."

Zack let the screen door slam as he hurried to the barn. Bubba crawled out from under the porch and trotted along beside him.

"Take care of the place while I'm gone, boy," he said as he patted the old dog. Bubba had been a faithful dog for several years.

He hitched Betsy to the wagon and was soon on his way to Clewiston. Bubba followed for a couple of minutes before tiring. Zack turned and saw that he was sitting in the dusty road, watching him.

The morning sun was pleasantly warm as Zack began to contemplate his time with Io. He envisioned her shiny, black hair hanging in two thick braids, and wondered if she was doing well selling her baskets and other crafts. Anxious to get to town, he flicked Betsy with the reins. "Let's go girl," he called and Betsy picked up the pace.

As they clip-clopped over the little wooden bridge and rounded a curve, the Clewiston Hardware and Lumber store came into view. Across the street was Taylor's Livery Stable.

After passing several houses, Zack was in front of Tinsley's Mercantile and Pharmacy. Pulling Betsy to a halt, he threw the lines over the hitching post and went inside.

"Howdy, Mister Tinsley."

"Mornin', Zack," Mister Tinsley mumbled.

Guess he's still his same old grumpy self, thought Zack.

"Ma needs a few groceries. I figured I'd get them before I get the lumber to repair the barn."

"Do you plan t' pay Miss Ruby's bill, too? She owes almost four dollars and it's been some time since she's been in to pay on it."

Glad that he had picked up extra money before leaving the house, he replied, "Sure, Mister Tinsley. I reckon I can do that."

He gathered the items his ma requested, then began choosing ammunition.

"You wantin' bullets, Boy?" Mister Tinsley asked with contempt.

"Yes, Sir."

"You ain't going to be like your pa, now, are ya, boy? Sheriff Cole said he killed some black logger and he's hiding out somewhere. That so, Zack?"

"I reckon so, if that's what Sheriff Red Cole said." He laid several boxes of shells and bullets, along with two of the largest door bolts he could find, on the counter beside the groceries.

"I need some locks for the windows, too," said Zack as he turned back to get them.

Mister Tinsley looked with exaggerated shock at the extra large pile of ammunition lying on the counter.

"You plannin' on a war, boy?" When Zack gave no response he continued, "Maybe you're gettin' all that gun fire for your pa. I hear there's a real bad gang back in these parts. Is your pa part of that gang, boy?"

Zack felt his neck and face flush in anger and wanted to punch him right in the face, but instead he continued standing without speaking or looking at the scornful store-owner.

"I heard they killed and robbed three families, somewhere up close to Orlando. You hear anything about that?"

Ignoring the statement, Zack said, "How much do I owe ya?"

Mister Tinsley picked up a pencil and added everything together. "With your Ma's three dollars and eighty-two cents, that will come to nine dollars and ninety-six cents."

"Let's make it ten dollars even. I'll take four penny's worth of candy for the young'uns. Just mix up the flavors. They don't get candy very often."

As Mister Tinsley handed him a bag of candy, Zack noticed him place the little slip of paper on which he had recorded his mother's account, back into the drawer behind the counter.

"I'd like Ma's ticket, too, please." Zack locked gazes with him for the first time since coming into the store.

Mister Tinsley looked surprised then muttered, "I didn't realize I had put it back in the drawer." He took the ticket out and laid it on the counter.

Without changing his gaze, Zack requested, "Write *paid in full*, please."

The graying man mumbled something Zack couldn't understand, scribbled *paid in full* on it, then handed it back to Zack.

Still angry about the slurs and accusations Mister Tinsley had been tossing, and feeling he now was in control, Zack requested, "Would you sign your name, please? I need to show Ma that I paid it." A tiny smile of satisfaction played across Zack's previously stern lips.

Mister Tinsley angrily signed his name and slapped the ticket into Zack's hand.

"Thank you, Sir," said Zack as he gathered his purchases. Carrying them to the wagon, Zack ran his eyes up and down the narrow street to search for Io. Not seeing her, he pulled himself onto the wagon and headed further into town. Soon he saw someone in colorful Seminole clothes with her back to him, but she was much larger than Io. He pulled up and stepped down from the wagon. When the woman turned around, he realized it was Io's mother.

"Hello, Zack." White Fawn smiled. "I haven't seen you in a long time."

"Mornin', ma'am. I've been loggin' with my pa." He paused and looked around. "Is Io in town today?"

"Well, now, that just might be according to who's asking," she answered as she glowed with a mischievous smile.

Zack realized he was blushing but looked her in the eye. "Well, I reckon that would be me. I've been lookin' forward to talkin' to her."

"She is across the road in that dress shop. I think people call that '*window-shopping*'. I expect her back any minute now." She paused, then in sincere tones she said, "We were very sad to hear about your father. I'm sure it is hard on your mother and you, as well as the other children. Is there anything we can do to help?"

"Thank you, but we are doin' the best we can. I don't reckon there's anything anybody can do."

"Well, Zack, we can pray for you."

"Thank you, ma'am. That will help."

Zack felt a touch on his sleeve and quickly turned to see Io's big smile and glistening black eyes. His heart began to beat faster and he suddenly wished her mother were not there.

"Hello." Io's voice was as velvety as he had remembered. "Uncle Billy Joe told me you were home. What are you doing in town?"

"I had to buy some supplies but mostly I wanted to see you," he blurted without thinking. "Your mother said you were window-shopping. Did you see something you want in the dress shop?"

"Oh, yes, several things, but they were all too expensive for us to buy. They have a wonderful silk scarf that I would love to have. Its turquoise and white with lovely pink flowers and green leaves–all different shade of pinks and greens." Her eyes danced as her graceful hands drew the imaginary floral design in the air.

Io stepped to her mother and they conversed for a few seconds in the Seminole language, then she turned to Zack. "We packed a lunch and would like for you to join us. There's plenty for all three of us."

"I ... perhaps... Well, I really don't want to intrude. I...I need to get on back home."

"Don't be silly, Zack. Mother and I insist that you share our lunch." Her tone seemed to settle the matter. "We were packing up anyway. Not very many people were interested in our baskets and crafts today, but we did sell some of our smoked fish. People like them. We have plenty left for our lunch, too."

"Let me help you pack your things," offered Zack.

White Fawn loaded his arms with a stack of colorful baskets while instructing him where to place them in their wagon. By the time he finished, the women were behind him, loading the rest of the goods.

"We want to go down by the creek and eat. Are you through with your shopping?"

"I still have to get the lumber we need to repair the damage on the barn, but I'll come back to get it after we eat."

"That will be good," White Fawn said as she climbed onto the wagon.

"Will you ride with me?" Zack asked Io.

"May I ride with Zack, Mother?" After a nod and slight smile from her mother, Io continued. "We will meet you at the creek."

Zack helped Io onto the seat and climbed up beside her. Placing his arm around her, he gave her a quick but meaningful hug. "I hope you don't mind, Io. I missed you so bad. I thought about you every day."

"Of course I don't mind, Zack. I have missed you, too." She scooted closer to him and placed her hand on his.

"You know, Zack, if you would come to church more regularly, we could see each other more often."

"I know that I should. I guess I have let things get in my way lately. Ma wants to come more often, but I'm not comfortable with those people. I think folks look at me as though I'm mean like Pa."

"That's your imagination, Zack. People know you're only responsible for yourself, just as your father has to answer for himself."

Zack thought for a moment then said, "I'll see you there Sunday."

"Is that a promise?" asked Io.

"Promise!" assured Zack as he squeezed her hand.

In silence, they drove the rest of the short journey to the creek.

Io's mother had the basket out of the wagon and was spreading food on a cloth under a large banyan tree. Zack saw the fish, flat bread, guavas and another wild fruit, but there were a couple of foods he didn't recognize.

"I'm hungry," Io declared as Zack lifted her from the wagon. They raced to the tree laughing and holding hands.

Io quickly sat on the ground and pulled Zack down beside her. After prayer, Zack's inhibitions disappeared. Maybe it was the company that made this the best food that he had eaten in a long time.

"Zack, I understand your mother is with child," said Io's mother. "Is she doing well?"

"She is looking very pale and gets tired real easy-like. I don't reckon I know how a woman is supposed to be when she's going to give birth. All I know about is how our animals act, and I can't tell they're any different until they start birthin', except they get real fat." As the women laughed, he wiped his mouth and moved away from the food.

"I reckon I got a lot to learn," he continued.

"Are you planning to come to church Sunday?" asked White Fawn.

"I'm sure Ma will want to come, so I reckon I'll bring her."

"If you're not in a hurry, let's go for a walk," Io suggested.

They walked toward the creek. Zack thought he heard the rippling water singing, or was that his heart?

Io picked a bright yellow-orange flower with a black center from a profuse patch of Black-Eyed-Susan's, and teasingly began pulling its petals, one by one. "He loves me... he loves me not... he loves me..."

Zack took the flower from her and continued, "He loves you... he loves you... he loves you, so don't forget it!"

Her frivolous laugh turned into a serious gaze. She wrapped her smooth fingers around his rough callused hand, which was holding the near naked brown flower center and stem. "I won't forget it, Zack," Io promised.

As their gaze locked for a few intense seconds, they both knew they were making an unspoken promise that they would always keep.

Silently they walked back to the wagons. Zack helped Io and her mother onto their seat.

"Thanks for sharin' your dinner with me. I really enjoyed it."

"Call me if your mother needs me to help with her birthing or for any other reason. I'll be glad to come, day or night."

"Thank you, ma'am. I'll tell Ma," answered Zack.

He watched as they drove back onto the road and crossed the little wooden bridge before taking the reins to go back into town.

Passing the lumber store, Zack went straight to the dress shop. He did not know the very attractive middle-aged lady inside and felt uncomfortable among all the feminine dainties. He had never been in a dress shop before. As she stepped closer to him, he noticed her wonderful fragrance and wondered what made her smell so good.

"May I help you?" she asked with a smile.

" Y-yes ma'am," Zack stuttered. "There was an Indian girl in here this morning. She was admirin' a silk scarf. Do you still have it?"

"Oh, yes," answered the clerk. "I'll get it for you."

In a moment she was back with the beautiful silk piece and handed it to Zack. Holding it, he was shocked by its weightlessness, and the fact that he could see right through it.

"How much?" he asked. He hoped he had enough money left to buy the scarf and the lumber he needed.

"That will be forty-seven cents."

Zack took a deep breath and counted his money. "I'll take it," he said.

She took the money, then wrapped the scarf in white paper and tied it with string before handing it to Zack. "Your young lady has excellent taste," she remarked.

Blushing at the phrase, *your young lady*, he smiled nervously and hurried to the wagon.

"Let's go, girl!" he commanded as he turned Betsy toward the lumberyard.

After purchasing the materials he needed, Zack slapped Betsy into a fast trot.

Chapter Eight

The Panther

Zack was looking forward to the trip home as Betsy clip-clopped noisily across the little wooden bridge. He imagined that he could feel Io close beside him. He drew a deep breath hoping that would stop the twitter inside his chest. His happy lips stretched across his face in an ardent smile.

"Betsy," he said to his beloved horse, "I think I'm in love!"

Soon, town was well behind him. The ruts deepened and the road narrowed as it wound through the tall pines, palmetto thickets, and scrub oaks. It was getting late. If he didn't hurry it would be dark before he got home and Ma would be worried.

He snapped the reins to encourage Betsy to move a little faster.

Zack took advantage of the quiet, peaceful clip-clop of Betsy's hoofs and the rumble of wagon wheels to think about his life. He wanted to feel that he was worthy of someday asking Io to be his wife, but how would she deal with his drinking problem? He certainly had not conquered it, but Injun Billy Joe's prayer in the barn that morning had definitely helped him get through the day.

He thought about how he first learned to read, by getting their Bible down and asking his mother to help him. Although Ma wasn't as educated as Pa, she could read well enough to teach him. Then, when Pa came home the first time, he taught him to read well. The Bible was his favorite book, and even now he often read the big

Family Bible that Ma kept on the buffet. It had belonged to William's family.

He also enjoyed Zane Grey's books. They pictured strong men with good morals. His father was a strong man but lacked good morals. Aunt Rita had given him several of her Zane Grey books, usually for his birthdays. They were used, and once in a while had a slight tear, but that didn't matter to him. He cherished each of them and had read them several times.

His mind went back to Io and his promise to go to church. *I still wish I could be like Peter or Paul,* he thought. *They were good disciples who always put Christ first in their lives. I wish I had the nerve to walk up to the altar Sunday and ask Parson Smith to pray for me. I know I can't live right and stop drinking without God's help. No, I'm sure I could never walk to the front of the church, 'cause all those people would stare at me.*

He rode on for a few minutes, thinking about the sacrifice that Jesus made to save man from sin.

After some serious thought, he said, "God, if you will make my legs hold me up, I will walk to the altar and give my heart to you."

Realizing he had just made another serious promise, he tried to get his mind on something else. As he rode, his thoughts rambled over everything from his mother and siblings to the big bear that roamed the neighborhood.

Soon they were almost home. Betsy followed the road around a blind curve, then reared straight up on her hind legs and whinnied with fear.

"Whoa! Whoa, Betsy." As Zack tried to calm her, he saw a large panther crouching, ready to attack. The afternoon sun reflected bright golden highlights where it played on his magnificent coat. He couldn't have been more than twelve or fourteen feet from them.

Tightening his grip on the reins, he tried to command a quiet but firm voice to reassure Betsy. If she were to bolt into the woods, the wagon would surely be wrecked and he would be vulnerable to the panther's vicious fangs and claws. Zack had seen a young girl who had been mauled and killed by a Florida panther. The memory sent chills down his spine.

Betsy's front hoofs shook the ground as she pawed and snorted. She began to back away from the threatening cat. The left wagon-wheel backed into a deep sandy ditch, landing with a jolt. The wagon bed scraped the sand with each of Betsy's fearful movements.

"Now look what you've done!" Zack said under his breath. The wagon was going nowhere.

A chilling scream filled the woods as the panther issued his warning.

Zack continued speaking calmly to Betsy, but his heart was racing. The panther took several deliberately menacing steps toward them and crouched again. The sleek, tan cat was now close enough that one leap could land him on top of Betsy, or possibly in the wagon. His tense muscles rippled under his shiny coat as he again threatened to attack. He curled his lips to expose mammoth white fangs, while the thick hair between his muscular shoulders stood straight up. His long whiskers quivered an additional warning as a prolonged, guttural growl issued from his wide opened mouth. In fear, Betsy renewed her efforts to back away, but the wagon was hopelessly stuck.

Not sure of what he should do, Zack stood and grabbed a long piece of lumber from the wagon bed. He thrust it toward the snarling animal, while flailing his arms and loudly commanding, "Get! Get out of here, *now*!

At the sound of his screaming voice, Betsy commenced to thrash between the traces, but Zack continued his noisy show of strength. The vicious panther began backing off the road. It looked like the animal was conceding the fight, but with another terrorizing scream, he came back onto the road and posed in a half-crouch, exhibiting one colossal paw with dangerously sharp, extended claws. Zack recognized this as a direct challenge, and knew that he must not show fear. He continued his barrage of yelling and poking a ten-foot piece of lumber toward the tan tormenter until the panther again backed off the road.

After slowly easing backward about six yards, the panther suddenly turned, and with two mammoth leaps, he bounded out of sight into the dense slash pine and palmetto thickets.

Zack replaced the plank and hopped from the wagon. "Now what are we going to do?" he questioned reassuringly as he stroked his faithful horse.

Betsy answered with a low snort and a bounce of her beautiful head, but her legs were still trembling.

Zack heard a panther scream in the distance and knew the threat was long gone.

The shadows were getting longer by the minute. Zack walked around the wagon examining the damage.

I have to find a way to get this wheel out of this hole, he thought. Suddenly he spoke aloud, "Oh, thank God, I bought lumber today!"

He pulled some of the wood off the wagon and tried to wedge a piece under the wheel, but the ditch was too steep.

"Come on, Betsy. Go, girl–go–pull!" Zack snapped the reins as Betsy pulled, but the wheels wouldn't budge.

Zack found a broken limb and begun the tiring task of digging the wheel out of the shifting sand. Slowly, he was able to work the wood farther under the wheel.

"O.K., Betsy. Don't let me down. When I tell you to pull, pull hard!"

After several strenuous attempts, Zack pushed with all his might as Betsy pulled. His rig was finally freed.

A sigh of relief escaped Zack as he wearily climbed onto the wagon.

Thinking about the encounter, his mind went back to his childhood when he and Billy Jake had a frightening episode with another Florida panther.

"Come on Zack. Come on. I want to go home." Billy Jake's babyish voice was irritating Zack.

The fish had just starting biting. "Wait a minute, Billy Jake. I just want to catch a few more."

"Pa's gonna be real mad if we're late. We ain't done our chores yet, either. Come on, Zack."

Billy Jake plopped down on the creek-bank beside Zack. "The mosquitoes and 'no-see-ums' are eatin' me up, Zack. Let's go, pleeease."

"Shut up and get still, Billy Jake. The fish ain't biting 'cause you've scared 'em away."

With a loud sigh of resignation, Zack's little brother tried to be still but was soon scratching and whimpering. "Come on, brother. I want to go home."

Zack realized it was almost dark and knew Pa would probably give them both a beating since they had not done their chores.

"All right, Billy Jake. Let's go. We'll cut through the woods. It's a lot faster."

The sun was already out of sight so the woods were becoming quite dark.

"I'll race you home, Zack." Billy Jake took off into the dangerous darkness with Zack right on his heals. The deer trail was barely visible as they twisted through the palmettos and pines.

Running into a tiny clearing, Zack heard a low growl. He grabbed his brother by the overalls to stop his forward movement.

"Shush-h-h." he quietly warned. "I heard a panther and it sounded real close."

Both boys froze with fear as they peered through the darkened woods.

Zack never did see where the panther came from, but there, not more than ten feet away, was the feared cat. He was frozen as still as Zack and Billy Jake in an apparent standoff.

"Don't look him in the eye," Zack instructed under his breath. "Slowly walk backward and stand behind me."

Obediently, Billy Jake did as he was told. The panther did not move.

I know you're not supposed to make eye contact, Zack thought, *but now that I'm already staring at him, the only thing I can do is hope he will decide to leave.*

Time slowed until thirty seconds seemed like five minutes. Zack could not detect any movement, but he suddenly realized the cat had melted into the pine thicket.

It was then that Zack noticed an acute pain piercing his side. He reached behind him and took Billy Jake by the arm in an effort to loosen his little fingers from his overalls--and skin.

Speaking softly, Zack said, "Walk slow now, Billy Jake. I think he's gone but he may be watching us from the trees. Just take slow steps and don't make any noise."

Billy Jake took two very slow quiet steps, then, his pent-up fear became *'un-pent.'*

"Maaa-maaaa!" His terrified cry rang long and loud through the woods. He ran as fast as his little legs could move toward the house.

Allowing his own fear to dominate, Zack followed. He imagined that he could feel the panther's hot breath on the back of his neck as he ran with all his might.

Their two new puppies, Bubba and Baby came running to meet them. The lights shining through their windows were a welcomed sight.

Boy, Pa whipped us good that night, Zack remembered, as Betsy pulled into the yard. Slowly, old Bubba came out from under the house and followed him to the barn.

The light shining through their window was again, a welcome sight to Zack.

Chapter Nine

Aunt Rose

Zack awoke to a tap on his window. Throwing the light blanket off his feet he moved close enough to see Injun Billy Joe, and hurried to the back porch.

Injun Billy Joe greeted him with, "Good morning. Were you planning to sleep in today?"

"Mornin', Billy Joe. What time is it?"

"It's almost five o'clock. Are you awake enough to talk to me?"

"Yes. What's the matter?"

"I think we need to go check on your Aunt Rose. I have been hearing some bad things about an outlaw gang. If it's who I think it is, they will surely make William Bentley's sister one of their first stops."

"I hadn't thought about that, Joe, but Mr. Tinsley did say they had robbed and killed some folks in Moore Haven."

"Did you get the ammunition you needed?"

"Yep, and I loaded every gun on the place. Do you think they will come here?"

"There's no way to know, but it's wise to be ready if they do." Injun Billy Joe straightened his knife scabbard then continued, "Is Miss Ruby good with a gun?"

Zack thought for a moment, brow furrowed and gently biting his lip. "It has been a while since Ma had to use one, but a couple of years ago two foxes got into the chicken yard. Ma stood on the back porch with a rifle and killed both of 'em. I reckon she's good."

Billy Joe flashed a quick smile. "I'm sure she can handle herself. I'll be back in an hour. Can you be ready to go by then?"

"I'll be ready. How long do you think we'll be gone? Guess I'll have to tell Ma what we're doin'."

"There's no way to know how long, but I'm sure you'll figure out what to tell her."

Zack opened the screen, and then turned back. "Billy Joe, do you think we need to bring Aunt Rose back here? I hate for her to stay in them woods alone."

Billy Joe thought for a moment. "Miss Rose is a proud and independent woman. I really doubt that you could persuade her, but you can try."

Zack nodded then went inside.

Ma's usually up by now, Zack thought. He started a fire in the wood stove and put the coffeepot on, then went in to check on his mother. She was dressed and sitting on the side of the bed.

"You feeling all right, Ma?"

"I'm just a little tired, son, but I'm alright. Why was Billy Joe here so early?"

"When I was in town yesterday, Mr. Tinsley said that outlaw gang that had been up around Orlando had come this way and that they had robbed several families in Moore Haven. They even killed some of them. Billy Joe thinks the leader might be the one that used to be in Pa's gang years ago, you know–the one that got away from Pa an' went to Georgia an' formed a new gang. That's who Billy Joe thinks it is, an' he…"

"Zack," Ruby interrupted. "Zack, how in tarnation did you learn all this? I've tried to protect you from your pa's doin's. I figured if you didn't know, it would be easier to raise you right."

"Ma, I have some coffee makin'. Let's go to the kitchen to talk."

Ma slipped into her shoes, and with strings dangling they headed for the kitchen. She opened the pie safe and took out a loaf of bread that she had made yesterday. Sliding the iron skillet over heat, she then dipped a spoon of hog lard into it.

"Pa told me about Aunt Rose, Ma, an' besides that, I'm getting too old for you to keep stuff like that from me. Pa took me by her place on the way here after he shot Big John."

"How did she look? Did she seem to be well?" Ruby queried.

"Well," Zack thought, then spoke slowly as he placed the plates around the table. "She's a real little thing, and she don't take good care of herself, but I reckon she's all right. I don't think she sees enough other people, so she's real lonesome."

Without answering, Ruby got busy stirring flour into the lard to make egg gravy.

"Ma," Zack felt reluctant and sheepish but definitely wanted to talk. "I want to ask you something about Io."

Zack's tone was so intense that Ruby turned to look at him. "What about Io?"

"Well, she and her mother invited me to eat picnic lunch with them yesterday. She is really a very special girl, Ma, an' she's so beautiful! Do you…I mean…well, how do you know if you're in love? Ma, I think about her most all the time, an' I want to marry her someday."

The big spoon clanged as it hit the edge of the iron skillet and then bounced onto the stove. Ruby spun around to stare at Zack, half laughing and half bewildered.

"Zack, where in the world have I been all the time you was growin' up. I still think of you as a young'un, and here you are thinkin' you're in love, even thinking about gettin' married!"

The smell of burning flour caused her to turn back to the stove where she resumed stirring.

"She is a pretty girl, Zack, an' she comes from a good family. I've known her mother several years an' she seems real nice, and of course, Billy Joe has always treated us like his own family."

Zack poured two cups of coffee and sat at the table. "Oh, yeah, Ma, I almost forgot to tell you that Injun Billy Joe and me are goin' to check on Aunt Rose. Do you think it will be alright if we bring her back here until Sheriff Red catches those crooks? I really do hate to leave her alone."

"Sure, Zack. Go wake the young'uns for breakfast. It would be nice to see her again, and she might be a lot of help when it's time for the baby."

As Zack pushed his chair away from the table it scraped the wooden floor. "By the way, Ma, Io's mother said she will be glad to help when it's time." His voice trailed off as he hurried toward the bedrooms.

Soon he returned and continued as though he had not been gone. "She said, just let Billy Joe know and she'll come. By the way, have you been making tea out of the herbs that Billy Joe brought for you?" He sat down, blessed the food and began eating.

"I've been out for a couple of days. Maybe that's why I'm so tired."

The children straggled in one by one with Harmony Belle coming in last, shoes and unmatched socks in hand.

Zack gulped down his last bite of biscuit and gravy and grabbed his hat off the nail by the door.

"I figure Injun Billy Joe will be here by the time I get Betsy saddled. I'll have him bring some more herbs, Ma."

"Billy Jake," Zack continued, "you an' JJ make sure you get the chores done and stay close so you can help Ma if she needs ya. I'm not sure exactly how long I'll be gone."

"Where ya goin', Zack?" Harmony Belle's babyish voice brought Zack back to plant a quick kiss on top of her curly head.

"I've got an errand to run. You stay close to Ma, will you? You stay close, too, JJ, 'cause Ma might need you for something."

"Billy Jake," he added with a hand on his brother's shoulder, "please try to get all the chores done but if you can't, I'll help with what's left when I get back."

"I want to go fishin' today. You ain't my boss, Zack."

"Maybe he's not, Billy Jake," Ruby spoke, "but *I* want you to stay close, too. No fishin' today. Now finish eating and get your chores done. You too, JJ."

"Don't worry, Ma," Zack reassured his mother with a big hug. "We'll be fine."

As he hurried toward the barn to saddle Betsy, the chickens noisily scattered and Bubba fell into step beside him.

"Hope you'll enjoy this little trip today, girl," he said as he gave Betsy a loving pat. Taking the reins, he walked her back toward the house.

JJ had come out and was sitting on the porch, playing the harmonica that Pa had brought to him when they came home from logging almost a year ago. Zack was surprised that he had taught himself how to play so well. He smiled and waved to his little brother as he hopped onto Betsy.

Billy Joe was waiting at the side of the house. His brown and white paint was pawing the ground impatiently. Soon the two friends were trotting northward.

"Billy Joe..." Zack hesitated.

"Is something bothering you, my friend?"

"I don't feel very good about leaving Ma and the young'uns alone, but I think I would feel worse if we didn't go to see about Aunt Rose. What if they do go to her house? Do you think they'll kill her?"

"There's no way to know, Zack. That is another one of those things we have to leave to God. We will do what we can but some things are beyond our abilities."

They rode in silence for a short distance then turned off of the main road .

"This is the same deer trail that Pa brought me on when we left Aunt Rose's place."

"Yes, it cuts off several miles. That's always good when you're in a hurry."

As they rode on a little further, Zack said, "I can't see any tracks except jack rabbits."

Injun Billy Joe bent over and studied the trail. "There are signs that deer were here yesterday, but there have been no horses on this trail since the last little rain shower."

They rode in silence for several miles. Zack's mind wandered from one thought to another.

After twisting a couple more miles through the woods, Billy Joe made a sudden stop. "That big red stallion belongs to Miss Rose."

Zack strained his eyes looking through the trees in the direction Billy Joe was pointing. "What stallion? I don't see a horse."

Billy Joe dismounted and pointed into a dense clump of trees. "He is off to the right of that tree that has a little sunshine on the trunk. Can you see that?"

Zack squinted. "I see it."

"Now look to the right between the next two trees. That big red is standing stone still. I'm certain he sees us, too."

As Zack looked, he realized the horse was almost in full view.

"I reckon I would have ridden right on and never knew he was there. How far are we from Aunt Rose's house?"

" Less than a half-mile," Billy Joe answered.

"I suppose that stallion might have broke out of the fence, you reckon?"

"Let's walk on," Billy Joe suggested after riding a little further. "He might follow us back to Miss Rose's place. I'm not real sure why he is out here in the woods."

Billy Joe took a deep breath. "I smell smoke."

They continued winding through the trees until they came to a clearing. Dismounting, Billy Joe began to study the sand.

Zack saw several hoof prints. "That horse must have spent a lot of time grazing this clearing. How long do you think he was here?"

"These tracks are not from your aunt's horse, Zack. They were probably made yesterday, and were made by several horses with riders."

The gray smoke was becoming thicker and lay in the trees like a dense fog.

Zack gasped, realizing what could have happened. "Do you reckon…?"

"We must not jump to conclusions, Zack. I think we'll leave the horses here and walk on to the house."

Zack followed closely behind Billy Joe until they could see the house roof. Kneeling down behind some thick undergrowth, Billy Joe put his ear on the ground. After a moment, he stood and whispered, "I don't hear a thing, but stay close to me."

As they neared the home place, Zack saw charred heaps of timber and ashes, some still smoldering, where a barn had stood. The air was filled with a sickening stench of smoke and seared flesh. Several chickens, pigs, and a cow strewed the ash heaps, obvious fire victims.

Moving cautiously, they were soon positioned on the back porch. Injun Billy Joe motioned for Zack to stay there and he slipped quietly through the unlocked door.

The few seconds Zack waited felt like minutes. Hearing nothing, he followed his friend inside. Shattered glass shone on the kitchen floor and table. Three wooden chairs were broken and thrown around the kitchen.

Fearing the worst, he started toward the front room but froze at the doorway. He had almost stepped on a bloody hand and arm. His first thought was that Aunt Rose was lying on the other side of that wall, but then he realized that the hand was much too large and fleshy to be hers. With great apprehension he eased his head around the corner and saw a man lying against the wall with a hole in his chest. The wood flooring was soaked with blood and some still looked wet. He was wearing an empty gun holster but there was a thirty-eight pistol gripped in his right hand.

The lovely deep red velveteen sofa, on which Zack sat when he was here with Pa, had been slashed. The room was totally trashed.

Zack's mind whirled. *I must find Aunt Rose*, he thought.

Cautiously he made a path to the bedroom. At first all he saw was severe vandalism, then, as he stepped further into the room he saw another body—another man. His head and one shoulder propped against a cedar chest. Zack guessed that he had been shot at close range, judging by the wound in his stomach. A hunting knife had fallen to his side and lay in a pool of blood.

"Oh, Aunt Rose, where are you?" he moaned. "And where is Injun Billy Joe?"

Hurrying to the front door, he opened it and stepped out. Billy Joe was squatting in the sandy dirt, reading horse tracks.

He stood when he saw Zack. "There were at least five horses that came in here, but it would appear only three rode away. Also, they left in a big hurry. From the tracks, it looks like the other two horses ambled into the woods."

"Have you found Aunt Rose? Something horrible happened here."

"Zack, we need to look around the place. I'm still hoping she is hiding somewhere." He momentarily let his eyes sweep the surrounding area.

"I don't think there is any more threat here. They have moved on, but we need to see if we can locate Miss Rose."

As they began searching, Zack said, "Who do you suppose killed those two men?"

"Not much way to know, Zack, but since they were each killed by a single rifle shot, I imagine Miss Rose shot them."

They walked around the corner of the house and Billy Joe continued. "I've been told that after they murdered her family, your aunt became one of the best sharp-shooters in south Florida."

"Do you suppose this is the gang that Pa told me about?"

"That would be my guess. I figure they broke in on Miss Rose since the lock was shot out, but I also figure she was able to kill those two before they got her, if they actually did get her."

"I didn't notice the lock," Zack said as he bent down to search under the house. "Aunt Rose!" he hollered. "Aunt Rose, can you hear me? This is Zack, William's son." The wide open crawl-space under the house proved to have no place for her to hide.

Zack noticed what looked like blood on the corner of the house, as if someone had grabbed it to hold themselves up.

"Look," he said.

Billy Joe looked, and then saw a track in the dirt and grass that led toward the smoke house, about seventy-five feet to the north.

"Something was dragged into the smoke house," said Billy Joe as they both rushed to the old building. It was locked from the outside.

As Billy Joe removed the wooden peg from the latch and opened the door, Zack pressed in beside him.

Immediately Billy Joe tried to push Zack back but it was too late. Zack had already frozen with horror as he gazed at the ghastly sight before him. His hands seemed to be glued to the door facing which his fingers gripped so tightly that Billy Joe could not pry them loose.

"Oh, God," Zack cried with a heart-rending moan. "What have they done to you?"

Aunt Rose's hands had been tied together. Her clothes were partially ripped from her frail body. Blood had poured down her frame from multiple stab wounds, and burn marks were visible on her arms and chest. She was hanging on a mammoth meat-hook, as flies buzzed noisily around her putrefying body.

Zack wondered how anyone could be so wicked! *Did they kill her after getting the information they demanded, or did they ride off and let her slowly die from this gruesome torture?*

Zack's head began to swim as nausea overcame him. He came to his senses enough to realize that Billy Joe was trying to release his grip and push him back through the door. Zack felt like he would lose his breakfast. He had never before seen such a chilling, terrifying sight.

Billy Joe shut the door and placed a caring hand on Zack's shoulder–a shoulder that was now slack with grief. "We'll have to leave her here until the sheriff can investigate, but I'll make sure she gets a proper burial."

"Why would anybody do that to an old woman?" Zack sobbed. "Why?"

"Only God knows, Zack, but I know that there will be a judgment day and God *will* hold them responsible."

"Do you think they were tryin' to make her tell them where Pa is?" Zack sobbed.

"That is quite probable but no one will ever know for sure," Billy Joe answered.

After a few silent moments, Billy Joe asked, "Zack, do you think you can pull yourself together? There is much that we have to do. Are you going to be able to help me?"

Zack took a deep breath, squared his shoulders and pulled his head up. "I made Pa a promise that I would try my best to take care of our family."

The picture of Aunt Rose again fogged Zack's mind. *I don't think I'll ever get that scene out of my mind*, he thought as he again battled nausea.

"I guess that promise included Aunt Rose," he continued, "but... "He tried to be brave, but his cracking voice betrayed his agonizing fear that he had somehow failed.

"Your pa would be proud of you, Zack," said Billy Joe. "I think the first thing we need to do is to find Sheriff Red. We're not too far from Clewiston."

They hurried around the house and into the woods where their horses were tied. Mounting, they rode as fast as the deer trail would allow, and were soon on the main road. Zack halted. "I think I should hurry home to make sure Ma and the young'uns are okay. What if those men were able to make Aunt Rose tell them where we live? They might be there right now."

Billy Joe nodded, "I think that's a good idea, Zack, but I really doubt they will show up at your place until after dark. I have a feeling that Miss Rose wouldn't give them any information, no matter what they did to her. They will probably split up and ask around for directions today. It might even be later this week before they get to your house."

"I'd like to believe they'll never come but I don't believe that's gonna' happen," Zack said.

"Did you get new locks for the windows and doors?" Billy Joe questioned.

"We sure did," Zack answered. "They might be able to break a window out but we would at least know they were there, and I don't think they can get into either door without shooting it down."

"That's good. Hurry on, now, and I'll be there as soon as I get through in town."

Before Billy Joe finished speaking, Zack had slapped Betsy into a fast run, headed home.

Chapter Ten

The Incursion

After putting Betsy in the pasture, Zack rushed into the house. Harmony Belle was sitting on the floor playing with the cat and her doll.

"Hi, Zack," she said. As she jumped up, Tom scurried across the room.

"Hi, sweetheart. Where is everybody?"

She put one hand on her hip and with the other she put a finger over her lips. "Shuush," she whispered through protruding lips. "Mama's asleep and she said for us to be quiet."

"Where's Jesse Jordan and Billy Jake?" Zack asked in lowered tones.

"They're outside. Mama told them to hurry and get their chores done."

"Well, you stay in here while I go find them. Don't go outside, even if somebody comes into the yard. I'll be back right away."

Zack fastened the new lock he had put on the front door, and then went out through the kitchen. Standing on the back porch he let his eyes meander around the yard before he went to the barn.

The boys were tussling in the hay and the chores were not finished.

"Hey!" Zack shouted.

Surprised, they came up from their wrestling, looking like scarecrows with hay sticking all over them.

"Zack," Jesse Jordan exclaimed. "I thought you was gonna' be gone all day."

"Yeah, Zack," Billy Jake offered. "We was just restin' before we finished the chores."

"How much more do you have to do?" Zack asked.

"Well, Billy Jake and me were gonna' share so the work would go faster."

"How much more do you have to do?" Zack repeated.

"We already slopped the hogs and gathered the eggs." JJ stood tall and seemed to be waiting for his big brother to praise him.

"JJ, I want you to go in the house and stay with Ma and Harmony Belle. I'll help Billy Jake finish the chores."

"Why?" questioned JJ. "I want to stay outside and play."

"JJ, do as I say," Zack ordered. "And one more thing," he stepped close to his little brother and lowered his voice. "The front door is bolted. Make sure you don't unlock it and don't let Harmony Belle come outside, no matter what."

Jesse Jordan cocked his head and wrinkled his brow.

"What's the matter, Zack?" he asked.

"Nothin's the matter. Just do as I say and make sure you don't wake up Ma."

Jesse Jordan went obediently to the house. Zack noticed Billy Jake staring at him with a concerned look.

"What's the matter, Zack?" he repeated his brother's question. "You look awful! Have you been crying?"

Zack took a deep breath trying to decide how much to tell Billy Jake. He realized his younger brother was a growing up fast, and that he could see that something was wrong. Zack knew he had to be honest with him.

"There is a gang of outlaws in this area and I think they might be coming here."

"How do you figure?"

"I heard they are tryin' to find Pa–it's about something that happened before any of us was born, but I'll tell you all about that when we get more time," he said. "Let's hurry and finish the chores. There are some things I need to handle in the house."

Zack pitched hay to the horses and cows while Billy Jake milked Minnie. She was known as one of the best milk cows in the area. Neighbors often came to Ma for milk when their cow was dry. Zack remembered when they first got her. He thought she was the most beautiful animal he had ever seen. The white spots on her shiny black coat were almost identical on either side, but he was always intrigued with her huge eyes and super-long eyelashes.

Zack threw out the last fork of hay and went to see how close Billy Jake was to finishing. He stood watching for a minute, then saw he needed about two or three more minutes.

"Zack," Billy Jake asked, "how long do you think it will be before Suzie's piglets will be born?"

"Shouldn't be much longer, Billy Jake. Injun Billy Joe said they should be here by the next full moon."

"I reckon that's about when Ma will have her baby, too," Billy Jake laughed. "They're both getting really big."

Zack laughed with him, "I reckon." He had never heard Billy Jake mention a new brother or sister before.

He didn't feel comfortable leaving Billy Jake alone, but he also needed to get inside and check on Ma and the young'uns. He also needed to place the guns where they could easily get to them if need be.

"Go on in, Zack," Billy Jake said. "I'm almost through here."

"Do you think you'll be all right? I really don't want you out here alone."

"I'll beat you in if you don't get goin'." Billy Jake grinned. One of the things Zack loved about his younger brother was the fact that when he smiled, his grin crinkled up his whole face.

With a light slap on his brother's head, Zack chuckled and hurried into the house.

Jesse Jordan was on his hands and knees, chasing a giggling, squealing Harmony Belle who was chasing Tom, the ever-playful black and white cat. Ma was in the big rocking chair, sipping a cup of hot herb tea. Her big smile told Zack that she was enjoying watching the children play.

"I told those young'uns to be quiet, Ma. Did they wake you up?"

"No, Zack. Until I came in, you couldn't hear a peep from them. In fact, I was worried that they were out in the woods somewhere." She took a deep breath and then, as if thinking out loud, she said, "I don't take time to enjoy their playing often enough." Her tender eyes spoke of her immense love for her little ones.

Zack went into his bedroom and began loading the guns. He noticed a shadow darken the light from the door and looked up. Ma was standing there, still holding the teacup.

"You came home a lot sooner than I expected, Zack. Tell me about your trip. I reckon Rose didn't want to come back with you. I didn't figure she'd want to leave the home place." She sat down in the straight chair by the tall, homemade chest-of-drawers that Uncle Bill Wheeler had made.

Forgetting that Billy Jack was still not in, Zack walked over to his mother and knelt in front of her.

"You look like you've been crying!" She placed a hand under his chin and pulled his face up.

"Look at me, Zack!" she commanded. "My Lord, have mercy," she cried out. "What has happened?"

Zack laid his head on his mother's lap and sobbed out the horrors he and Injun Billy Joe had seen at Aunt Rose's place. Ruby gasped, instinctively placing her hand on her protruding belly as if to protect her unborn child.

"Ever since Billy Joe first talked to us about them working their way down here I figured it was the one outlaw that your pa didn't get. He said his name was Buck…Buck…oh, I can't remember his last name, but your Pa said he was the meanest one in the bunch. He said there was nothin' he wouldn't do. They're headed here, Zack, you can count on it."

"Ma, do you think Pa would have done bad things like that bunch did to Aunt Rose...I mean torture and kill a poor old woman like that?"

"Zack," Ruby assured, "your pa did some very bad things, but he never did anything like that. He had a sense of justice that would never let him do something like that. He told me lots of times about keeping his gang from that kind of meanness."

After a moment of silence, she asked, "Do you think we can handle it, Zack? Can we protect the babies and our home from those murdering outlaws?"

"We have to. If they are trying to find Pa, they might be here tonight or tomorrow, but we *will* have to fight. Ain't no way out of it."

Zack quickly finished loading the guns he had in his room. "Ma, here's plenty of shells. Go to your room and get your rifle. I think we have enough shells and bullets here to just about hold off an army.

Ma went to her room and soon returned with her gun. As she loaded it, she asked again, "So do you think we can handle it if... when they come."

"We have to handle it, Ma," Zack repeated, "and with you, and me and Billy Ja...," Zack felt blood drain from his face as he thought about what could happen to his younger brother.

"Ma, have you heard him come in? He should have come in already."

He stepped from his room and realized the children were much too quiet. Foreboding came over him as he eased toward the front room.

Surely something is wrong, he thought with alarm. Tilting his head around the door, just for a second he saw the petrifying situation.

Motioning for Ruby to stay away, he eased her back to the bedroom.

"Ma, they're here!" he whispered. "I saw two of them. One of those brutes has brought Billy Jake in. He is sitting at the table with a gun to his head."

Ruby gasped as the color drained from her face. She tightened her grip on her shotgun and said in low tones through clenched teeth, "They can't come in here and hurt my children!"

"Shush, Ma, think this through. If you go in there with a gun, he'll probably pull the trigger and kill Billy Jake." She thought for a second, and then asked, "Where are JJ and Harmony Belle?"

"The best I could see, they were sitting on the floor beside Billy Jake." Zack felt an ache in his chest as he thought about the fearful expression on Billy Jake's face and hated himself for leaving him outside alone.

Now he was faced with many decisions. He knew that no one had seen him. They would have to quickly decide how to handle this.

"You find a way out to go get help," Ruby said with resolve, "and I'll go in and keep things as calm as possible until you get back."

"Ma," Zack said with concern, "I can't leave you and the young'uns here alone!"

"Do as I say, Zack," Ruby said as she headed toward the front room.

He knew she had already made her decision and arguing was not an option.

Zack thought for a second and realized all the windows were nailed and bolted shut. Breaking the glass would alert the crooks that he was there. The only way out was to finish pulling up those loose planks under his bed. He had gone out that way several times when he was younger, but he was much bigger now. After filling his pockets with shells and securing his gun in his belt, he quickly and skillfully moved the bed, taking care not to make any noise. Since they had never been fastened back in place, the floor planks came up easily, even one that hadn't been moved in years.

Zack shifted the high iron bed back over the escape, slid under the bed and deftly slipped through the hole. Lying on the ground he worked as fast as possible to place the floor planks back over the opening, hoping they wouldn't be noticed.

Rolling onto his stomach, he searched the surrounding yard. He could not tarry too long, but knew he must be careful. He had only seen a small portion of the kitchen, but he knew they would surely have one man posted outside as a lookout. Three horses were under the big oak tree, loosely tied to the old swing. Zack knew he had to locate the third outlaw before he could go for help.

Listening carefully, he heard voices in the house, one being his mother's, but could not make out what they were saying. Silently he prayed, *God, this is one of those times that I really need your help. Please let me know what to do.*

Just then he heard footsteps on the back porch and realized he could not get to Betsy without being seen. Thinking for a moment, he decided to take one of the outlaw mounts as they could not be seen from the back porch or the kitchen.

Cautiously staying low he eased toward the horses. *God, please don't let them snort. You know they're my only hope.*

As he approached the horses, he spoke softly, hoping they would stay calm. He removed the loosely looped reins from the swing and slowly led them toward the road. Dusk was setting in. Miraculously, the big animals made no sound as they followed Zack. He never even heard a twig snap under their hooves.

Having taken all three horses, he wondered why, as he needed only one. *Well, since I have them,* he thought, I *guess I'll ride one and leave the others down the road a ways.*

Glancing back to make sure he had not been noticed, he mounted a big mare and, leading the others, he slowly made his way toward Clewiston. As soon as he thought their hoof-beats would be out of ear shot, he slapped his mount on the rump as he said, "Get!" The mare bolted, and Zack almost hit the dirt. He had been used to riding Betsy, a small horse. This big animal showed him some power.

Holding tightly to the other two horses' reins, he rode a little farther. Knowing they were far enough that the outlaws would not be able to find them, he let go. They rapidly fell behind as he kicked his mount to go faster. The wind zipped through his too long, curly hair, and his worried mind kept pace, zipping from question to question. *What if he couldn't get help in time? What if the outlaws discovered their horses missing and decided to kill one or all of the family? What if...*

Zack caught himself worrying and remembered his promise to go to church Sunday and give his life to Jesus. *You've brought me this far, Lord, now please take care of Ma and the young'uns.* In spite of his fear, Zack felt an extraordinary peace come over him as darkness fell.

He rounded the next curve, and came face to face with Sheriff Red and Injun Billy Joe. A posse of three riders was close behind. They pulled their horses to a halt and Zack was pleased to see that the tall thin man he disliked was not among them.

In as few words as possible, Zack told all that had happened, then turned his prancing mare around.

As soon as he had a clear picture of the situation, the Sheriff broke into a fast run. Zack was glad he was riding a horse that could keep up.

When they got to the place where Zack turned the horses loose, the Sheriff stopped. Both animals were standing in the nearby trees. He and the posse decided to walk their horses a little further and then leave them tied to a tree, going the rest of the way on foot.

"Just try to make sure that Ma or the young'uns don't get hurt, Sheriff Cole," Zack pleaded as he remembered the atrocious things they did to Aunt Rose.

"We'll do the best we can, son, but this isn't a very good situation to work in." The sheriff's words were surprisingly compassionate, as though he felt Zack's pain.

"I'll go to the back and see if the lookout is still there," offered Billy Joe. "If he is, I'll take him out. Then we will only have to deal with the two inside."

"That's good," the sheriff answered. "The rest of you men spread out around the house and ease in as close as possible. Zack, can you get back in without them knowing?"

"I'm pretty sure I can, Sheriff. It might take me a couple of minutes longer now. I'll have to go much slower." Zack knew the task would be a dangerous one as he would have to feel his way in the dark.

"What do you want me to do when I get back in?" he questioned.

"We'll have to figure that out when we see what is going on in the house and where everyone is," the sheriff answered.

Soon the house was in sight. Zack's heart began to race, fearing the worst.

"All of you wait here until I go in and survey everything," offered Billy Joe. "I'll come back and we can make a plan.

"Sounds good to me," they all agreed.

"That sounds like a good plan, Bil…" The Sheriff was speaking to the Indian, but he had already vanished.

The men stood quietly waiting for Billy Joe to return. Shortly he was back with all the information they needed.

"The man Zack saw on the porch was at the barn, getting ready to burn it. I had to kill him," he said matter-of-factly. "Everyone else is in the kitchen. One man is eating and the other one is trying to make Miss Ruby tell him where William is. I saw him hit her once, and then he threatened to kill the children if she wouldn't talk."

"We have to move fast, men. Zack, go back in and if you can get to the front door without being seen, unbolt it so we can come in." As Zack moved toward the house, the Sheriff continued, "Son," his tone stopped Zack, "don't let your anger make you do something that might endanger yourself or your family. No matter what happens in there you must not react in the wrong way. Now go, and God be with you."

Zack was determined to prove that he was mature enough to do a man's job. He hurried toward the house and crawled underneath. Feeling his way, he soon came to the metal box that marked the right spot. Reaching up he slowly removed the boards until there was enough room to get through.

As he lay under the bed, he heard Harmony Belle crying. He heard a slapping sound, followed by a loud hateful, "Shut up!" She screamed, and continued the loud howling.

"Mama," he heard her whimper.

"Can't you see your mama can't help you, girl?" the rough voice yelled. "Can't you see she's busy telling old Buck where your rotten Pa is hidin'?"

Hatred welled up in Zack. If it hadn't been for the Sheriff's admonition to control his anger, he knew he might have rushed in to save his sister. He also knew it would have been disastrous.

Zack tried to shut out all the horrible sounds coming from the kitchen and concentrate on the task at hand. He was glad to see that the front room was dark. It looked like the lamp on the buffet had been broken. Glass glistened in the light from the kitchen doorway.

He reached the front door and prayed that no one had seen him. Gently he pulled the large bolt back and then turned the knob. The door opened enough for the Sheriff to know he had done his job. *Now,* he wondered, *what am I to do?*

He moved away from the door, and the bare-footed sheriff slipped inside, followed by two bare-footed posse members. They eased toward the kitchen where abusive sounds were abundant. Zack held his breath and tightened his jaw in anger as Buck again slapped Ruby.

"I know you know where William is hidin'," he yelled. "You've got one minute then I start shootin' these here little ones."

"I *really don't* know where he is," Ruby sobbed. "I would tell you if I did."

The back door flung open and Injun Billy Joe appeared, followed by the other deputy. Simultaneously Sheriff Red, along with the other two men, bolted from the front room, through the breezeway, and into the kitchen. Before the man at the table knew what had happened, Billy Joe knocked him to the floor. At the same time, he seized the gun from the table. The blow obviously knocked the man unconscious, and he lay on the floor beside Billy Jake.

The other outlaw grabbed Ruby around the neck with one arm while holding his pistol in the other hand, and began backing toward the wall. Red streaks marked Ruby's face and her clothes were bloody and torn.

JJ picked up Harmony Belle and swiftly moved to the front room to get her out of the way.

Zack's long arms instinctively surrounded his two sobbing siblings, but his ear was glued to what was happening in the kitchen.

"Where's Billy Jake?" he asked.

"That man at the table got mad and hit him in the head with his gun." JJ seemed fearful and Zack noticed blood on his shirt.

"Are you hurt?" Zack asked. "Where did that blood come from?"

"I ain't hurt. That blood is from Billy Jake," he answered. "I went to him and tried to help, but that mean man made me move back."

Rage again seethed in Zack. "JJ, take your little sister to your room and stay there until I come for you."

They ran toward the hall as though they were glad to get as far as possible from the hellish ordeal in which they had been trapped.

Zack went into the kitchen where Billy Jake lay without moving. Kneeling beside him, he lifted his head. Billy Jake was bleeding from the large gash in his head, but Zack saw that he was alive.

Leaving the last outlaw to the Sheriff, Zack grabbed a towel and poured a dipper of water in the wash-pan. As he knelt beside Billy Jake, he looked up in time to see that Billy Joe had somehow gotten behind the outlaw who was restraining his mother. Before Buck could release Ruby to defend himself from the fearsome Indian, he was dying with Billy Joe's long hunting knife in his heart.

Ruby fell to the floor along with the outlaw, Buck.

Two deputies quickly carried Buck's body into the back yard. Sheriff Cole handcuffed the outlaw who had just started to come out of his unconscious stupor.

When the deputies returned, the sheriff gave them custody, and they promptly pushed his staggering body through the back door.

Zack did not know what had happened to his mother, so he left Billy Jake to rush to her.

"Zack," she said faintly as she laid her head against him, "it's over. Thank God it's over."

"Ma, are you okay?"

"I'm just tired and scared, son. That scoundrel… that animal even threatened to," she hesitated as her body quivered with repulsion, "he threatened to rape me here in front of the children! "Oh, Zack," she cried with a hand over her face, "I was devastated!"

Billy Joe picked up a chair, which had been overturned in the ruckus, and then he and Zack gently lifted Ruby into it.

As his mother began straightening her torn clothes, she asked, "How is Billy Jake?" Before he could answer, she continued, "I'm all right, Son. Just take care of Billy Jake."

"He has a gash in his head where that brute hit him, but I believe he will be fine," Zack reassured.

"That filthy thug that kept hitting me was the only member of William's old gang that was still alive. His name was Buck Bailey. Your father told me about him shortly after we married. He said that he knew he would someday have to deal with him, too."

"Since Pa was not here, as usual," Zack said bitterly, "*we* had to deal with him."

Injun Billy Joe was taking care of Billy Jake. "He will be all right, Zack. Get some of the herbs I brought for your mother and some clean cloth to bandage his head. He'll be up and going in no time."

After pouring fresh water in the basin, he cleaned Billy Jake's wounds then bathed the dirt and blood from his face and arms.

As Zack knelt beside his brother, Billy Jake opened his eyes. "Zack," his voice sounded weak. "Just as I was coming in with the milk, they rode in. I was caught in the middle of the yard and… and before I could get to the house, he had a gun against my head. I couldn't yell or warn you 'cause he would have killed me." Billy Jake began to cry. "I'm so sorry."

Zack spoke reassuringly, "It wasn't your fault. I should have never left you out there alone, but I didn't think they would be here this soon. Can you ever forgive me?"

Billy Joe interrupted. "Let's get some clean clothes on Billy Jake and your mother and try to get them in bed. This has been a terrible ordeal for them."

"I want to wash up first," Ruby said. "I feel so nasty. That filthy pig had his hands all over me."

"Of course, Miss Ruby. Zack can take care of Billy Jake, and I'll get you a pan of warm water."

Zack helped his brother stand on very wobbly legs, then pushed a chair under him.

Sheriff Cole, who had been sitting quietly at the table, said, "Before I go, I need both of you to answer some questions if you are up to it."

"What do you need to know?" Ruby asked. Zack was always amazed at his mother's inner strength.

"Did they talk to you at all about where they had been or what they have been doing?"

"They bragged about killin' *old woman Rose*, whoever that is," said Billy Jake. "They acted like I should know who she is, but I never heard of her before."

"What else did they say?" he asked.

Ruby spoke up, "They said that they were from Georgia, but the sheriff up there was getting too close on their trail so they decided to try their luck in Florida. They also said they wouldn't have any trouble killing all of us, because they had already killed several families around Orlando and Moore Haven."

Sheriff Cole listened intently before saying, "Miss Ruby, I am very sorry for you and your family, but I know that it could have been much worse if you had not kept your senses about you."

Turning to Injun Billy Joe he said, "We were glad to have your help, Billy Joe. The Bentleys are lucky to have a friend like you."

"Well," said the sheriff as he stood, "If you don't need me any more, I'll go. I have a long night ahead of me with bodies to contend with and a prisoner to process."

He started through the door, then turned back and said, "Zack, I was pleased with the way you handled yourself today. You showed a lot of strength and maturity. Just keep going and you will soon become a fine man."

Zack acknowledged him with a nod and a faint smile as he left the house.

"If you don't need me, I'll be going, too," said Billy Joe.

After seeing that his brother was comfortably in bed, Zack stepped into the front room. He could hear water sloshing and decided to give his mother privacy as she bathed. He could hear her muttering and moaning under her breath but couldn't understand her.

He went to her room and found a housecoat. "Ma, here is your housecoat," he offered.

Ruby reached her hand around the door. "Thanks, Zack."

In another minute she came through the room, trying to keep the housecoat closed over her huge belly. "I really need some sleep, Zack, and so do you. I'll see you in the morning."

"Night, Ma. I'll lock up."

"It has been a hard day, Son. I never could have imagined this happening. I love you, Zack, and I'm so sorry you had to find Rose and go through that agony." She bent over and kissed his forehead, then went to bed.

Chapter Eleven

The Camp Car

Zack was far too stressed to go to bed. Mechanically, his eyes scanned the room for a bottle of whisky. Not finding one, he eased his fatigued body onto the sofa and rested his head in his shaking hands.

I have gone several days without a drink, he thought. *I guess it's a good thing there is no liquor here now or I know I would give in.*

He removed his boots, and then lay back on a soft sofa pillow. His mind wanted to peruse the events of the day, but he knew that would be more trauma than he could handle.

He longed for an earlier period in his life, when things were not so complicated. *Even the times that I thought were bad, were better than things are right now,* he thought.

With eyes closed and a deep sigh, Zack thought he could clear his mind and maybe even

go to sleep. Instead, his thoughts went back to a time, shortly after his father came home from prison.

Zack sat on the ground making a 'road' in the clean-swept yard. After Pa came home from the big red building where Zack had first met him, Pa made a little wooden wagon with wheels that really turned. It was painted bright red, and Pa had written Zack's name on it with white paint. That was the best toy he ever had. He was happy to sit for hours building roads in the sandy dirt and driving his cherished toy on them.

Zack also listened to the conversation between Ma and Aunt Rebecca as they sat on the front porch, rocking and talking.

"William is really trying to keep his promise to me and the children," Ruby was telling Aunt Rebecca. "He hasn't been drinking at all, but I can tell he really wants to."

"Well, as long as he takes care of you and the children and doesn't beat you around like he used to, he'll be all right with me."

Zack wasn't sure what they meant by drinking. Everyone he ever knew drank. *I love to drink water from the dipper,* he thought. *It feels so nice and cold, and I really like it when Ma makes cold tea.*

Ruby continued. "Zack will be six next week. I would like to do something special for him. He really is such a good young'un."

"Why don't we give him a little party before you leave?" Aunt Rebecca asked. "We could have Rita bring her four and we could have a nice party."

"That sounds wonderful," Ruby said with excitement, "but right now we don't have the money to bake a cake or to buy a present."

"Well, I'll bake a cake," offered Aunt Rebecca, "and all that will really matter to Zack will be having the other children here to play for an afternoon."

"Well, all right," Ruby agreed reluctantly, "but I'll have to ask William first."

Zack didn't really understand what a party was, but it sounded good. He enjoyed it when his cousins came to play.

He pushed his little wooden wagon further away from the porch and was soon caught up in the things he loved, building roads, pushing twigs into the soft sand to make fences, chasing butterflies, and playing with roly-polys. It delighted him to see the little hard-shelled dark gray bugs roll into a tight ball when he touched them.

That night while eating, William announced, "We'll be leaving day after tomorrow."

The women caught their breath. Rebecca said sadly, "Oh, William, I had hoped we would at least have a week or so together. We just got here yesterday."

"There's a camp car available day after tomorrow, and the Hosford Lumber Company is hiring now. I signed up to leave Wednesday. We'll be logging from Okeechobee to Bithlo, and over on the west coast from Old Town to Perry. Then we'll probably go on up to Bay County in the Panhandle."

"Well," said Uncle Sam, "it looks like you won't run out of work, William."

"I don't suppose we will, but one thing is sure, if we don't leave now, I won't get the job, and the pay is better than it is around here."

Ruby frowned, "I just don't know if I can be ready to go that soon, William."

Zack thought his father looked angry. "You won't have to pack much, Ruby. There's not much room in that tiny car. Just pack clothes and things that we have to have. Everything else we need, we can buy from the company store."

Rebecca looked at Ruby and said, "I reckon we won't be having a party for Zack."

Zack noticed his father glare at the women, but he said nothing.

After supper that night, Ma started packing her things.

Zack stood in her doorway for a few moments…then asked, "Ma, are you leaving us? Where are you going? Will Aunt Rebecca be our Ma?"

"No, Zack," she explained. She looked shocked that he could have thought that. "You are going, too."

She knelt beside him and said, "We are all going to live in a camp car for a while so we can be with your Pa while he is working."

"What's a camp car?"

"Well," she explained, "do you remember seeing the train when we went to the big red house, the first time you met your pa?"

Zack remembered. "There was a lot of black smoke and it made a loud '*choo-choo*' noise, and had a real loud whistle."

"That's right, Son. We are going to live on one of those train cars as long as the logging holds out. Uncle Sam and Aunt Rebecca are going to live in our house and take care of the horses, and the cow, and the pigs, and keep everything nice until we come back home."

"Can Billy Jake come with us, Ma?"

"Of course he can, Zack. He's part of our family, too." Ruby gave Zack a reassuring hug. "Go get ready for bed and I'll soon come in to help you say your prayers."

Two days later, Pa loaded the wagon and they all left the homestead. Pa and Uncle Sam sat up front, and Ma and Aunt Rebecca rode in the wagon bed with the two boys. Zack noticed that Ma was crying again, and thought Pa must have done something to her.

"Don't cry, Ruby," Aunt Rebecca said. "A year will be gone before you know it, and you'll be back on the home-place. "We'll take care of the place as though it was ours."

Soon they were pulling up to the train tracks. Zack was excited to see things he had never seen before.

"Pa, look at those big cows!" he said excitedly.

"Those are not cows, boy," said Pa. "Those are oxen."

Pa and Sam walked to one of the railroad cars that looked different. Zack watched as a very tall, fat man came out and shook hands with them. After a couple of minutes, he pointed to a big huge box with a couple of windows in it.

Pa and Uncle Sam walked back to the wagon and William said, pointing to the same big box. "That's the one, Ruby. We'll pull the wagon over there and unload all our things."

Pa walked beside the wagon as Sam drove around to the opposite side of the big box. He pulled the wagon up close and halted. There Zack saw a door and another window. This all seemed very strange to him.

They went inside. There were two beds, some drawers, a table with chairs, and what sort of looked like a kitchen.

"Well, I reckon this will be home for a while. I think it will do just fine," William said, looking around the room.

Ma tried to smile, but Zack knew she was not very happy. "How big is this, William?" she asked.

"Well," he reflected, "I think I remember that they measure twelve by thirty feet."

Pa went to Ruby and put his arm around her shoulder, hoping to reassure her. "Do you think we can do it?"

"At least we can all be together," she said with a glimmer of a smile.

After the wagon was emptied, Ma and Aunt Rebecca set about putting things in drawers that were made with a frame that was nailed to the wall.

Zack and Billy Jake sat on the bed and watched. Zack tried to imagine what it was going to be like to live in that little house.

Soon Pa and Uncle Sam came back and Pa announced, "We have to get out until it's loaded on the flatcar."

Everyone went outside. The wagon had been moved away from the house and a team of six oxen was tied together, two, then two, then two standing on the opposite side of the train. Then they were hooked with big cables to the side of the box that was going to be their house. There were two very long skids there, one end was wedged under the box house, and the other end was up on a flatcar.

A man yelled to the oxen and they began pulling the camp car up the skids and onto the flatcar that was on the railroad tracks. It took a while, but their new house was finally sitting on top, like a part of the train. A short ladder was placed at the door and used like steps to get in and out.

"They will be pulling out soon," Pa said. "Thanks for all your help, Sam."

Zack watched Ma say goodbye to Aunt Rebecca and Uncle Sam.

"Zack, be good and help your mommy a lot," said Aunt Rebecca as she hugged both boys. "We will be here when you come back home."

They climbed up the ladder into their temporary home. It felt very strange.

Zack heard the big engines start and the shrill train whistle blow. Soon there was a lunge and then a clacking sound. Then a bigger lunge accompanied by a louder *clack-rattle-click* as the train began slowly moving. The boys ran to the window to wave goodbye to Aunt Rebecca and Uncle Sam, who watched, waving, until they went around a curve and could no longer be seen.

Pa stretched out on the biggest bed and Ma sat beside him. Zack and Billy Jake sat down in the floor and pulled a couple of toys out of a bag that Ma had packed for them.

At first they felt an occasional bump and heard a loud clack as the train started slowly moving over the cross-ties. The bump, bump, bump, followed by a loud clacking noise got faster and faster as they picked up speed, and soon they sat on the floor laughing. As they sped up, the bump-clack of the cross-ties tickled their bottoms. Their new house rocked back and forth as the train made its way around curves and up and down small inclines. The two boys rolled as their new house rocked. Sunlight flickered off and on as they passed the big trees growing beside the railroad tracks.

Finally, Billy Jake became sleepy and Ma put him on the smaller bed. Before long he was in a deep sleep. Zack heard Pa snoring, too.

Ma took her crocheting from her sewing box and soon her needle was flicking in and out of soft yellow yarn.

Zack pulled up a chair to watch Ruby crochet. "What are you making, Ma?"

"Well, Son, you are going to have a little cousin in a few months. Aunt Rebecca is going to have a baby and I'm making a baby sweater. I just hope we come back home before the baby is too big to wear it."

Zack didn't know whether to be happy or not, but he decided that, for now, it was more important to watch the trees and occasional farmhouse as they sped by.

Feeling very sleepy, Zack crawled onto the bed beside his little brother and was soon asleep. Later, he woke up and figured it was the middle of the night as his pa was still snoring. Moonlight flickered through the trees with enough light to see that Ma was lying beside

Pa and Billy Jake was still asleep beside him, so he closed his eyes and slept.

Awaking, he was happy to see Ma fixing something to eat as he was very hungry.

Pa was sitting on his bed.

"Are you about ready for breakfast, Zack?" he asked.

"I sure am hungry, Pa."

"It's almost ready, Zack. Get Billy Jake up for me."

The meal consisted of food they had brought from home, but it sure tasted good.

In time, the train began to slow down and the whistle was blowing very loudly. It blew one long and two short whistles. Zack thought that must be its way to say hello to the people who were there waiting for them. He ran to the window but could see nothing but trees. Soon the wheels were squealing with harshly grating metal wheels on metal tracks as they slowed the long train and finally came to a very bumpy stop.

Pa opened the door. The late morning sun glistened on his black curly hair with a golden glow. "They'll be unloading us soon, Ruby," he said as he climbed down the ladder.

As Ruby picked up Billy Jake, she said, "We have to get off. Zack, follow me and we'll watch them unload our house." She sounded cheerful as she carried his little brother down the ladder that Pa had put in place.

They walked a good distance from the train. Zack noticed several other camp cars lined up. Children were playing around them, and some of the older ones stopped to watch their new neighbors unload.

Zack looked for the oxen, but instead, there was a team of eight mules to unload the camp car. It seemed to Zack that it took hours to get the skids in place and hitch the mules to the camp car with thick metal cables.

Finally the house was on the ground and the mules pulled it into line with the other camp cars that were already there.

When their car was set up, Ruby said, "I guess this is it," and led Billy Jake inside.

Zack stood outside, watching the other children play. Some were playing tag and two others were swinging a long rope in a circle. One of the girls ran into the turning rope and jumped every time it hit the ground. As she hopped, her long blond braids would fly up in the air. They all laughed when she missed the rope and fell to the ground. It looked like fun.

Zack noticed a boy about his age watching him. As they smiled at each other, Zack felt that this boy would be his friend. They started walking toward each other and then stood smiling for a moment.

"My name is Ross," offered the redheaded boy.

Zack smiled and nodded. Ross seemed to be a little older than he.

"What's your name?" Ross queried.

"Zack," he answered, not sure how to act.

"Want'a play marbles?" he asked, pulling a small cloth sack from his pocket.

Zack shrugged. "How do you play?"

Ross sat on the ground and drew a circle in the dirt. He then poured small, colorful glass balls into the circle, removing two that were larger than the others, he handed one to Zack. "Here's a shooter for you. We call them *bullies*."

Zack tried to absorb the instruction being offered, but kept an eye out for his father, as he was not sure William would approve of his talking or playing marbles.

He held his shooter just like Ross did, trying to learn to shoot, but he just couldn't make it go more than a couple of inches.

He realized that someone was standing behind him, and then he heard Pa say, "Well, now, you seem to be having a problem." He took the big bully marble from him and instructed, "Zack, if you hold it in your other hand, it will be easier for you to shoot, because you're left-handed like me. This young man must be right-handed."

Zack was relieved that Pa was not angry. He put the *bully* in his left hand and was delighted as he shot it into the circle. Before long he was happily shooting the smaller marbles out of the circle, almost as well as Ross.

As dusk was setting in, Ma called him for supper.

"Can we play again tomorrow?" Zack asked as Ross placed the marbles in the little pouch.

"Sure, tomorrow's Sunday and we can play all day if we want to."

"I'm glad you've found a friend already, Zack," Pa said. "That's Ross Green. His pa and I have logged together before. He seems to be a good boy."

Happy that Pa had approved, Zack smiled and said, "Yes, Sir."

"It doesn't look like we'll be here more than a week or two at the most. Most of the timber has been logged out in this section." He cut a bite of fried sow-belly and chewed a couple of times before continuing.

"The company boss said they were heading north, probably to Hosford. They are paying more up there. I'll average four cents a tree here, and they are paying five cents up there in the panhandle. If my partner and I cut a hundred trees a day, that will be pretty good money. We might even be able to save a little."

The next ten days were quite enjoyable as Zack spent most of his time with Ross and the other children.

Moving time came and Zack was anxious to go to a new place but didn't want to leave his new friend. "Ma," he asked, "can Ross go with us?"

"They are going up there, too, Zack. Most of these camp cars will be moved on this train."

It took the better part of the day to load all the camp cars on the flatcars. The boys watched a while and played a while. Later that afternoon they were on their way to a new place.

The train rattled on, stopping here and there for more firewood and people, but the loggers and their families stayed in their camp cars. They rode all night and all the next day and the next night. Zack wondered if they would ever get there, but finally, the big metal wheels began screeching on the metal tracks.

"This is Hosford," Pa said. "I'll go find out how soon they will unload."

There were more people at the Hosford camp. As soon as they were settled, Pa and one of his friends left. Zack could tell that Ma was very unhappy but she didn't say anything.

Sometime later, Zack was awakened by loud arguing.

"William," Ruby's tone was low but she sounded troubled, "here you are drinking again, after you promised you wouldn't."

"Don't start that holier-than-thou mess, Ruby." His words were distorted and slurred. "It won't hurt a bit for me to have a little drink with my friends, so just shut up!"

Zack turned over in fear and forced himself to go to sleep.

From then on, things were not as pleasant as they had been. Ma and Pa fussed a lot and Pa would often hit Ma or him, or even Billy Jake for the smallest thing. Zack wished Pa would go away again and leave them alone, but that didn't happen. More and more, he came in drunk and Zack did everything he could to stay out of his way.

They stayed at Hosford almost seven months, until the timber was cut in that area then moved to a Panhandle logging camp called Bear Creek.

After Pa cut timber for a few weeks, they gave him a job rafting the cut timber down Bear Creek to North Bay. Zack heard Pa tell Ma that he had to attach cork to his shoes so he could maneuver the logs while riding a raft. He used spiked poles called *peavies* to guide the logs through the water to prevent jamming. Ma said it was real dangerous work because the logs could jam if the rafters did not keep them floating on the water properly, and they could be squashed to death.

Pa worked at the Bear Creek camp for about three months, and then he decided to go back to south Florida.

After an awful fight one night, Pa hit Ma so hard that her nose and mouth were bleeding.

"I'll just send you and the boys back to the homestead," William yelled. "Maybe that will make you happy."

Zack watched his mother as she laid her head on the table and sobbed. "William, can't you just stop drinking so we can stay together?"

"Why don't you just shut up! I'm sick of your nagging." With that Zack watched his pa storm out, slamming the door behind him.

Within a week, their camp car was hoisted onto a train headed back to Cross City, and then home. Zack never figured out how they knew to meet them, but Uncle Sam, Aunt Rebecca, and a three-month-old baby boy met them at the train station.

JJ came through the front room to get a drink of water. "Zack," he said, "Why are you still awake?"

"I guess it's just been such a horrible day with those outlaws and all. I needed to unwind a few minutes, but I'm about ready for bed now." His stomach and hands had stopped jerking.

He went with Jesse Jordan to the kitchen and noticed a blood stain where the slain outlaw had fallen. One of the deputies had cleaned most of the mess, but had somehow overlooked this one.

"JJ," Zack said, "hurry on back to bed. I have a couple of things I need to do before I go."

JJ took a few sips of water before going to his room.

Zack quickly cleaned the remaining blood from the floor, straightened the table and chairs and then went to his room.

Chapter Twelve

The Change

Saturday came with the promise of a sunny, beautiful weekend. Ma was scurrying around, getting their clothes ready for church.

"JJ," she said, "I need you to find shoe-black and clean up our shoes so they will look nice for tomorrow."

Jesse Jordan heaved a big sigh and slowly scooted his chair away from the breakfast table. "How come Billy Jake can't do it?" he grumbled as he went toward the bedroom.

"Ma," Zack said thoughtfully, "I know I promised Io that I would go to church Sunday, but the closer it gets, the more I don't want to go."

"You've never minded driving us to church before, Zack. What's your problem now? Are you upset because Io asked you to promise to go?"

Ruby carefully studied his face.

"It's not Io, Ma, it's…it's God!" Zack blurted out honestly. "I promised God that if he would help us get through this week, I would go to church Sunday and give my heart to Him." Zack propped his elbows on the table and leaned his head on his fist. Breathing deeply, he blew out a very long sigh. "I'm afraid I can't live the way He expects me to live. If I mess up and get drunk, or cuss, then everybody will feel bad at me and think I'm not trying to do right. But even worse, what if I do something bad and God won't hear my prayer anymore? "

Zack blew another deep breath and continued. "Ma, you know I've tried it before, and I just can't be good."

"Oh, Zack," Ruby turned around to face her distraught son. "If you give your heart to God, you won't have to use your own power to live right. Jesus will be there to help you. If He hadn't helped me I couldn't have come through this week and still kept my sanity. God was a constant comfort through the abuse Buck and his thugs dished out to me and the young'uns. He gives you His wonderful strength when you can't live right by your own strength."

Zack thought for a moment. "You mean Jesus can stop me from doing the bad things I want to do, like drinking, or losing my temper, or cussin'?"

"That's what I mean."

"But, Ma, you know I don't have much patience when things go wrong, or sometimes I cuss at the young'uns."

"Zack," Ruby said as she joined him at the table, "do you remember when we lived in the camp car?"

Zack looked up with surprise as he had just relived that experience in his memory, just three nights ago. "Sure, Ma."

"Then, do you remember the wood fire they kept burning in the train engine that made the steam and gave power so the train could keep running?"

"Sure, Ma," Zack seemed baffled. "Pa explained all that to me."

"Well, Zack, think back. What did they do when the wood car was about empty?"

"They stopped and the big loader would fill the wood car again," Zack said, "but what does that have to do with me living right?" Zack was perplexed.

"Did they ever run out of wood?" she continued.

"No, Ma'am."

"That, Son, is just the way God operates. When you have used up all your own patience, or love, or kindness, He just brings in His big loader and refills you with the patience, or love, or kindness that is supplied by Jesus. He always has more than you could possibly need. He has never run out of those things we need to live for Him, and He said that He will give us freely from His abundant supply."

Zack felt like a light had come on inside his head and a smile broke out on his face. He bent over his mother to give her a hug before leaving to do the chores.

"Zack," Ruby called, "get that washtub down that's hangin' on the porch. These young'uns have to get a bath for church tomorrow."

Zack reached up and got the old washtub and set in into the kitchen. *How many times have I filled this old tub for washing clothes and for baths?* he wondered.

The next morning the sky was just light enough to see when Zack awoke. As he dressed, he remembered it was Sunday. *This just might be the best chance I'll get to give this scarf to Io,* he thought as he laid the tiny white package next to his church clothes. The scent of frying salt pork and hot biscuits drew him to the kitchen, where Ma was getting ready to fry eggs and make gravy. "Good morning," she greeted.

"Morning, Ma."

"Did you rest O.K.?"

"Yes Ma'am."

"The coffee's ready. How about pouring some for the two of us."

Zack heard a noise and looked down and saw his sleepy little sister pulling out a chair. "I want some, too, Zack"

"Girl," he said as he pulled her curl, "you're too little for coffee."

"Mama lets me have it."

Zack looked quizzically at Ruby who smiled, "I'll fix hers the way I always do."

"I like a lot of sugar and milk in mine, Zack, and I don't like it hot."

Billy Jake and JJ came in looking sleepy-eyed. JJ plopped into the closest chair.

"Get out of my chair," Billy Jake demanded.

JJ didn't move.

"That's my place! Get up."

JJ didn't move.

"Ma, JJ's in my place. Make him move."

"JJ," Ruby said quietly, "why are you sitting in your brother's place?"

" 'Cause there ain't no chair at my place."

As Ruby set the gravy on the table, she asked, "Where is the other chair?"

"It's in the front room, Ma," said Harmony Belle.

"Why is it in there?" Zack asked.

"Me and JJ had it in there playing like it was the Ca-clu-ca-cat-chee bridge, and Tom was the boat that was goin' under it." Harmony Belle tilted her head and turned both palms up as if to say, *everyone should know that.'*

They laughed and Ruby told JJ to go get his chair.

As he left the table, JJ retorted, "Not Ca-clu-ca-cat-chee, Harmony Belle, it's Caloosahatchee."

Soon after breakfast was finished, the chores were done and everyone was dressed in their best clothes.

Knowing Io would be there, Zack made sure not to forget the scarf he had purchased. Maybe he could find a time to give it to her.

Zack had hitched the horse to the wagon and had it waiting in front of the house. He looked at his siblings with pride as they piled into the wagon.

Though his nerves were a little steadier, Zack still felt uncomfortable.

Many had already gathered at the church when they arrived. Zack glanced around to see if Io and her family were there yet but did not find them.

Ruby and the young'uns climbed down and started walking toward the church. Unsure of himself, Zack sat there, holding the reins.

"Are you coming, Zack?" asked Ruby.

"I'm going to take Betsy around back where she can be in the shade. I'll be in soon."

As he was positioning Betsy underneath a large banyan tree he noticed Io talking to one of his best friends, Dale O'Bannon. He immediately thought they were much too close, and he didn't like the way they were laughing. His first thought was to leave, but about that time, Io saw him.

With quick steps, they both came to the wagon.

"Good morning, Zack," Io's eyes were smiling as were her beautiful lips.

"Hello, Zack," said Dale as he offered his hand.

"Hello, Dale, how are you?"

"Io was just telling me that you were supposed to be here today. It's real good to see you."

"It's nice to see you, too, Dale." Obviously he had jumped to the wrong conclusion, thinking Io was flirting with Dale. A genuine smile broke across his face.

"It's almost time for church to start," said Io. "Pastor Smith hates it when we come in late." She placed her hand in Zack's, and they walked up the eight steps into the sanctuary. It was built high to withstand flooding from Lake Okeechobee.

Zack looked at the seating as they went inside. The only place that was left was a bench close to the front, just in front of his family.

Across the isle Zack saw Mister Tinsley and his wife. He hesitated. Anger welled up in him as he remembered the remarks Mister Tinsley had made right after Pa left. Io looked up at him, so he said, "I don't think I can walk down in front of all these people, and there ain't…isn't anywhere else to sit."

Dale took the lead and Io gently tugged on Zack's hand. "Hurry, Pastor Smith is about to start," she whispered, ignoring his hesitance.

About the time they were seated, the choir director said, "Please stand and sing page one-thirty-four."

Zack stood, noticing his legs felt weak, but as they sang, he became so engrossed with Io's melodious voice, that he forgot his trembling legs.

After a moment, he began listening to the words;

… … … He will carry you through.

Shun evil companions, Bad language disdain;

God's name hold in rev'rence, Nor take it in vain;

Be thoughtful and earnest, Kind-hearted and true,

Look ever to Jesus, He'll carry you thru.

It almost seemed to Zack that that song was chosen for him.

Songs were sung, prayers were prayed, and then the sermon was preached. Zack heard parts of it, like, *The Lord is good, a stronghold in the day of trouble; and He knoweth them that trust in Him.*

Zack began to remember how God had answered his prayers, as recently as this week. In his heart he knew that his entire family could have been killed, had God not been there to help.

His attention was drawn back to the minister who was quoting; *For I will forgive their iniquity, and I will remember their sin no more.*

God, if you will help me, I will try to make it to the altar like I promised, Zack thought.

The preacher said, "Please stand as the choir sings."

Obediently, Zack stood.

"There are some in this sanctuary today that could have been in the grave, had our merciful God not protected them. A terrible thing happened here this week, but you can be sure that God was in control of it all."

Zack realized he was talking about the outlaw gang and the trouble they caused. Zack remembered the promise he had made while in the midst of trouble--that he would give his heart to God if He would help him and his family survive.

As the choir began to sing, Zack's fingers gripped the back of the seat in front of him until his knuckles were white. *If I try to walk up there in front of all these people, I'm sure I will pass out,* he thought.

He listened to the words they were singing;

'Careless soul, why will you linger

Wand'ring from the fold of God?
Hear you not this invitation?
O prepare to meet thy God.'

He felt Io place a hand on his arm and she whispered, "I'll go with you."

He managed to loosen his grip on the seat in front of him and made a slight move toward the aisle, but couldn't seem to go any further. Then an arm was placed across his shoulder and Injun Billy Joe said, "This is your time, Zack."

Zack took one cautious step then another, and after seven steps, he fell, sobbing, at the altar. Billy Joe knelt on one side of him and Io on the other. Pastor Smith stood on the opposite side of the altar, in front of him.

Everyone around him sounded like they were praying out loud, but all he could hear was his own sobbing words, "Jesus, I have been so terribly wicked. Please forgive me for all my sins and, Lord, please keep my wood car full."

When he finished praying, he continued to kneel, silently thinking about the fact that he had just given his heart to Christ and what it would mean to him. He almost felt that if he stood to leave, the wonderful peace that had settled over him would disappear.

After a moment he realized that the weight he previously felt in his chest really was gone. His fear had given way to great joy and he began to laugh. No one had ever told him he could be this happy. He felt totally clean and forgiven. *I wonder if this is how Paul felt when Ananias prayed, and God gave him back his sight?*

He stood and Pastor Smith said, "Son, do you feel like God has done something for you today?"

"Yes, Sir," he answered as he shook the pastor's hand.

With this, Pastor Smith whispered close to his ear, "We need to talk later, Son. There's something about a *wood car* that I really don't understand."

At first, Zack was confused, and then he realized what he had said when he was praying. "Okay, Pastor, just tell me when."

He turned around to leave and realized his mother was right behind him. He turned and gave her a hug and whispered, "I feel so much better, Ma."

Her tearful smile was the only response he needed.

When they went outside, Dale said, "Zack, Io said that her mother will be in town this afternoon, visiting friends. She thought that since I am going by your house to take my mother to my grandma's house, maybe I could drop your family off so you and she could spend some time together. I'd be glad to do that if you want me to."

Zack was stunned. "That would be great, Dale. Are you sure you won't mind? Will you have room?"

"I'm absolutely sure, Zack. Just the two of us came to church today so there's plenty of room in the wagon."

"I didn't think I had seen Mr. O'Bannon anywhere. He couldn't make it today?"

"He didn't come in yesterday. They say they're really getting good hauls of fish right now. I'm sure Pa will stay out until his boat's loaded, and I know we could use the money," Dale said.

Ruby and the children climbed into the O'Bannon's wagon and were soon out of sight.

Zack and Io walked around the church to the banyan tree. Betsy seemed anxious to go.

They rode to the front of the church where Io's mother and Injun Billy Joe were sitting in their wagon.

"Don't stay out too late. Be back to Mrs. Faircloth's before dark, Io," her mother said.

Zack felt as though he was riding on air. The wagon seat was still hard wood, the streets were just as bumpy, and Betsy pulled the same, but he felt euphoria that he couldn't explain.

There had been something, almost like an ache, deep inside that was no longer there. The pain and guilt he had felt had been replaced with light-hearted exuberance, and, of course, he was thrilled to know that Io was seated beside him. He reached for her hand, which lay on a Bible in her lap.

"Are you hungry?"

"A little," Io admitted.

"Would you like to stop at the store and get something for a picnic, or stop at the restaurant?" Zack asked.

"The restaurant?" she questioned. "The only restaurant I know about is the tavern."

Zack immediately felt guilty. "I'm sorry, Io, I didn't think."

"Oh, don't fret over it. Let's stop at... Zack," she said with surprise, "this is Sunday! No store is open today, not even the tavern."

Laughter seemed so easy. Zack wondered if everything was going to be different now that he was a Christian.

"Let's go sit at the lake for a while. That's one of my favorite places, and then I'll take you back to Mrs. Faircloth's so you can eat."

"That sounds great to me."

They trotted along, sitting close together, and saying almost nothing until the expansive blue water appeared.

Zack lifted Io to the ground. As soon as her feet touched, she broke into a fast run as she called back, "I'll race you to that big rock."

Zack secured Betsy to a tree, and then started after her. Running as fast as he could, he gained very little. When he reached the rock, she was perched on top of it, laughing.

"You cheated," he chuckled as he jumped up beside her. "You had a head start."

"Oh, well," she said smugly, "that's the only way I can win."

The sun had warmed the rock, and it felt good.

This will probably be the best time I'll get to give Io this scarf, he thought.

He pulled the tiny white package from his pocket and handed it to her.

"What's this?" she inquired.

"Open it and see."

Quickly she tore into the paper, and gasped. "Oh, Zack, you bought me that scarf I loved so much. How did you know which one I wanted?"

"I asked the lady in the store which one you were admiring, and she brought it to me."

Io threw the colorful silk over her raven black hair, "Zack, I don't know what to say. Thank you so much!"

She stretched up and gave him a quick kiss on the cheek. "It's beautiful. I'll keep it as long as I live."

Zack knew he was blushing, but he really didn't care. That kiss was worth it to him.

For the next few minutes they delighted in a little teasing and 'small talk', then a thoughtful quiet ensued.

One of Zack's dreams, ever since he could remember, was to be able to work on a fishing boat. One of the few decorations in their home was a painting of a very large fishing boat. The water was churning, the wind was whipping the sails and the waves, but the boat seemed safe. Over his years, Zack had loved that painting and often told his mother that someday he was going to work on a boat like that. He knew that Lake Okeechobee offered many families a good living, although it was a difficult life.

"Since Pa's not here to make a living, I have been trying to figure out what I can do to support Ma and the young'uns." Zack's mood had become somber.

"I was eighteen this month, and if I could get a job now…" thoughtfully he paused. "I hate the idea of leaving Ma and the young'uns, especially after all that's just happened, but I reckon that's one threat that'll never bother us again."

"What kind of work do you want?"

"I'm thinking about asking Harley O'Bannon to let me work with him on his boat. I learn real fast and I'll work hard."

"That sounds good," Io interjected. "He seems to like you, and I'm sure Dale will put a good word in for you."

"I'll speak to Ma about it," said Zack. "I want to know how she feels, too."

Io leaned closer and laid her head on Zack's shoulder.

He slid his arm around her and was totally content to sit and listen to the gentle movement of the water.

They slid off their rock perch and walked toward the docks. One boat had just come in and they were unloading the catch. Hand in hand they watched for a few minutes.

"Look," Io was pointing toward the lake.

Squinting, Zack saw another boat heading in. They leaned on the dock rails and watched. The craft was making good progress. Before long one of the hands threw a rope to the dock keeper who tied it off. The crew quickly prepared to unload.

Zack listened to their conversation and knew that they had a colossal haul.

"If we're going to get to Mrs. Faircloth's before dark, we should be going," Io commented.

Zack felt a sadness that this day, probably the best day of his life, was about to end. They walked in silence to the big tree where Betsy stood waiting.

"I know you're hungry and thirsty, girl," Zack comforted as he rubbed her nose. "I'll give you water at Mrs. Faircloth's house, and you can eat all you want as soon as we get home."

She gave a soft whinny, as if she understood.

Mrs. Faircloth was a simple but very likable woman. "Come on in," she called as they arrived. "The food is still on the table and there's plenty of it."

"Thank you, Ma'am, but I need to get some water for my horse, if you don't mind."

"The well is in the back yard and you'll find a bucket hanging on the back porch. When you're finished, come on in."

Betsy was appreciative of her drink. When Zack went back in, the women were laughing and seemed very happy.

Zack said, "I think I had better go on home. I'm sure Ma will be starting to worry."

"Not until you eat," Mrs. Faircloth insisted. "Besides that, I have a question for you. I couldn't get Io to answer, but maybe you will." She pulled out a chair and pushed Zack down.

"Now, I've been knowing for a long time that you two were sweet on each other," she blatantly stated.

Zack felt his face getting hot, and when he looked at Io, her face was red. She had her eyes downcast and her fingers partially covered her smiling lips.

Mrs. Faircloth good-naturedly continued, "Is this getting serious?"

Zack was embarrassed. "We are too young to be serious yet. We'll let you know when we're older."

Mrs. Faircloth began to giggle and confessed, "That's what we were laughing about when you came in, Zack. I love to see Io blush."

Zack hungrily devoured a great meal, and then stood. "Thank you, Mrs. Faircloth, for the dinner. You're a wonderful cook."

"Zack, you are welcome here anytime," she said warmly.

Io walked to the wagon with Zack. "I've enjoyed the day, Zack, but what I'm most pleased with is that you have experienced that wonderful *change* that Christ makes in a life." She took his hand and said, "Stay in touch."

"You can count on it, Io." He wanted to kiss her magnificent lips, but, instead, he gave her a quick hug and bounded onto the wagon. Without looking back, he flicked the reins.

The change, he thought. *That's what I've always needed to make me different than Pa or any of our logging friends. That change has made me truly happy.*

Chapter THIRTEEN

New Life

Days passed. The circuit preacher came to Clewiston every other week, so Zack had attended services twice since he gave his heart to Jesus.

Pastor Smith finally found the right time to have a talk with Zack.

"Zack," he began, "I have been most anxious to talk with you about your prayer that Sunday morning that you gave your life to Christ. Please explain what you meant by, *keep my wood-car full.*"

Zack felt his face flush and he uttered a nervous giggle.

"Yes, Pastor Smith," he said, "I'll try to explain it like Ma explained it to me."

With great detail he told the story of his earlier life when their family lived in a camp car, and how he watched many times as they refilled the wood cars to make sure there was an abundant supply.

"You know, Pastor, I never did see them run out of wood. That engine always had plenty to keep it going. That's the way Ma explained to me that when I need patience, or love, or peace, or joy, Jesus is always there to supply me with all that I need."

After a moment Pastor Smith broke into a hardy laugh.

"I've never heard it put like that before," Pastor Smith said as he slapped his knees, "but that's a good illustration. Maybe I can use it sometimes to help others understand the abundant grace and mercy of God."

After a few more good-natured comments the pastor said, "Zack, have you considered water baptism? There are several others who have requested to be baptized."

Zack thought for a moment, then said, "I really hadn't thought about it, Pastor, but I have read in the Bible that folks were baptized after they repented."

"If you're interested, I will be doing the service before it gets too cold."

"I am interested, Pastor Smith, but I would like to wait until after Ma has her baby. I'd really like for her to be there."

"That's good, Zack, I would like that, too."

"Pastor Smith," Zack squirmed, trying to phrase a strange question, "do you… is there… well, do you think it's possible for me to someday be a preacher?"

Pastor Smith studied Zack for a moment before answering. "Do you want to be a preacher, Zack?"

"I'm not educated like you are, even though I read real good, and arithmetic comes easy for me, but I don't know if I can talk in front of all those people."

Pastor Smith sat quietly as Zack struggled with his thoughts. His face became more furrowed as he realized the seriousness of his words. "Everybody knows I'm William Bentley's son, and they all know he has… he is… I'm afraid they will think I'm like him, but I really try to do right."

Both men were silent for a few moments as Zack tried to put his true feelings into words. "Pastor, the answer to your question is, *yes!* I want to do something for God, but I don't know if I can be good enough."

"No one is good enough, Zack. We have to trust God and have faith in His Word. That means that when we become Christian, God looks past us and our human frailty, and sees only the blood of Jesus, His Son."

"Pastor Smith, do *you* think I could be a preacher?"

"Yes, Zack, and I believe you *will* go into the ministry someday." He answered as if he had been expecting Zack to ask that question. "When you gave your heart to God, I had a strong feeling that you had the calling on your life. Sometimes God will let me know those things so I can help prepare that person for God's work."

After a few more minutes of pleasant conversation and becoming better acquainted, they shook hands. Zack left with the very distinct feeling that they would become great friends.

As the days passed, Zack was happy to go along with life as it was, but the money Pa left was running low. He had to get a job very soon.

Since he had always wanted to work on Lake Okeechobee, maybe he could get hired on to one of the big fishing boats.

He and Ma discussed his getting a job, and they agreed that he should wait until after the baby was born and Ruby was back on her feet.

"I hate to lean on you so much, Zack, but since your pa's gone, I have no one else that can help."

"I'll do anything I can, Ma," he said.

Jesse Jordan bounded up the steps onto the porch and through the kitchen.

"JJ," Ruby scolded. "How many times have I told you not to slam the door?"

"Sorry, Ma," JJ said. "I just came in to tell you that my big red hen has a bunch of little fluffy yellow babies follerin' her around. I never could find her nest but I knew she was nestin'. Come see, Ma."

"I'm glad you could finally get a breath, JJ," laughed Zack.

"We'll be out in just a minute, son," Ma smiled.

A neighbor had given the hen to JJ when she was a tiny chick. He had kept her in a box in his room until she was big enough to run in the yard with the other chickens. Zack was glad he had something to make him so happy now, after the recent trauma.

Walking toward the barnyard, Ma said, "I want you to take me and the children to Aunt Rita's house, Zack. This will probably be the last time I'll feel like riding for a while."

"Sure, Ma," Zack answered, "when do you want to go?"

"Tomorrow," she answered as she pushed Bubba out of her way.

"Are you sure you're up to it?" Zack stooped over to pet his faithful red hound. "Last Sunday when we went to church, the ride seemed to bother you."

"Don't worry about me, son. I'm fine."

The next morning Zack slept later than usual. As he opened his eyes, he heard his mother urging the children to get dressed for Aunt Rita's house. He hurriedly dressed and went to the kitchen.

"What is all this food for, Ma?" Zack asked when he saw the extra food she had prepared.

"I just don't want your Aunt Rita to do it all herself, and she may not be prepared for company," she explained.

Before long the chores were finished and they all loaded into the wagon. Zack thought it looked like rain. Ruby agreed, but assured him that she felt the weather wouldn't be too bad for them to make that short trip.

"It's still early enough that we should be there in plenty of time for dinner," Ruby said.

"Ma," laughed Billy Jake, "you brought enough food for us to eat dinner and supper!"

When they rode into Aunt Rita's driveway, Zack noticed that colorful leaves were beginning to dot the clean-swept yard. His cousins were running across the porch and around the yard playing tag. Zack drove the wagon to the back where a long breezeway separated the kitchen from the rest of the house. As soon as they stopped, Jesse Jordan and Billy Jake jumped down to run and frolic with their cousins.

"Boys, get back here and help carry this food in," called Ruby.

Zack helped his mother from the wagon and noticed her grimace as her hand went to her low belly.

"Are you gonna be all right today, Ma?" Zack asked.

She assured him that she was fine. "I've been having little pains like that for over a week now. I'm sure it's just normal pain."

As they carried the food up the steps, Aunt Rita came to the door, grinning and drying her hands on her apron.

"Goodness gracious," she exclaimed as she took a large pot from Ruby. "I'm so glad y'all are here. I was afraid I wouldn't get ta see ya before the baby comes, since it's so close an' all. This is a real treat!"

After greetings were exchanged and the wagon was unloaded, Zack unhitched the team and put them inside the grassy area by the barn. He went into the breezeway and washed his hands. Ruby was saying, "I knew I would be stuck at home for a while, and I wanted to see you. How have you been?"

Aunt Rita opened the cabinet and got out a very tall stack of plates.

"I've been just fine, Ruby. Here, Zack, make yourself useful and set these plates around the table."

"Ma, can we go play now?" asked Harmony Belle.

"Yes, but don't leave the yard. We'll eat soon."

"Have you been able to put in your garden, Aunt Rita?" asked Zack.

"I put turnips and mustard in last week. I hope they'll make real good. I plan to plant the rest in two or three more weeks just before winter gets here. The moon should be right again by then."

Aunt Rita had always been a little bit chunky. One of the things Zack remembered from his earliest childhood was watching his aunt cook. Now as she stood at the stove stirring a big pot, Zack couldn't help but grin. Just as he remembered, her chubby bottom wiggle-waggled from side to side as she stirred, as though it had a mind of its own.

"Lee Roy Larson came by this morning," said Rita, "and told me that confounded bear was at it again. That rascal took his new calf and two little pigs."

Ruby began putting bowls of food on the table as she said, "I would hate for him to get into our barnyard. We sure don't have enough stock to spare."

She set a big platter of fried chicken on the table and continued. "Suzie is ready to drop her piglets any day now. I'd hate for that big brute to get any of her babies."

"I know," answered Rita as she jabbed the ice pick into a big block of ice. "Lee Roy said his tracks were enormous. He is getting more and more brazen, coming right up to the farms again."

"Something has to be done about him real soon," said Zack. "He'll have one of the children next."

Zack took a dish from his mother and placed it on the red and white-checkered tablecloth. "Injun Billy Joe said that some of the villagers had seen him when they were out collecting herbs. They said he was the biggest bear they had ever seen."

"Well, now," said Aunt Rita faking a shiver. "Thoughts of that monster give me the creeps. Let's think happier thoughts."

They finished loading the table and poured the sweet tea.

"Zack, call the children," said Rita. "I know they are all hungry by now."

They ran in, stopping at the big wash-bowl filled with fresh well water and after swishing their hands, they dried them on the clean white towel, leaving streaks of dirt.

Aunt Rita held up the towel, and then laughed as the children found their places at the table. "Here, Harmony Belle," said Aunt Rita as she placed a cooking pot upside-down on the chair. "This should fit just right." She lifted her onto the pot, then bent over and kissed the top of her curly head.

Taking her place at the table, Aunt Rita prayed a simple prayer of thanksgiving and then passed the plate of cornbread to Billy Jake.

"Ruby," Rita continued, "if you need me, I'll keep the young'uns while you're down."

"Oh, thank you, Rita, but I believe we will be just fine. Zack will be there and I'm really not worried." She took a bite of the chicken leg that she had been waving as she spoke. "I really do appreciate your offer though."

When they finished the last bite of guava cobbler and the little ones had run back out to play, Zack helped clear the table before going outside. There was a large spreading oak in the front yard. Its yellow, brown and orange leaves were falling faster than before. The wind seemed to be stronger. He brushed the leaves out of one of the heavy cedar lawn chairs that had been under that oak ever since he could remember. While sitting there his thoughts went to the recent conversation that he had with the circuit preacher.

How would Io feel about my wanting to be a preacher? Would she be willing to sacrifice to be in the ministry with me? How would Ma and the young'uns make it if I were not there to keep the homestead running? And finally, and perhaps most important of all he wondered, *what would happen if I were to give in to the strong, secret desires for whiskey that grip me from time to time? Am I really strong enough to control them?*

As he thought, he wished he had talked to Pastor Smith about the formidable urges he dealt with so often and wondered if God would also help him overcome them.

As the warm October wind became stronger, more leaves showered down until the clean-swept, sandy yard was no longer swept clean.

Zack realized they had better be heading home. The sky was looking more and more like they were liable to get caught in a downpour. He took a deep breath and could smell rain in the wind.

On his way inside, he passedt JJ playing hide and seek and told him to get the other kids ready to go.

"Can't we play just a little longer, Zack?" asked Harmony Belle who was hiding behind a small bush up close to the house.

"I'm afraid not, Harmony Belle. It looks like we'll probably get wet as it is." He pulled out the watch that Pa had given him for his fifteenth birthday, and was surprised that he had sat under the oak tree thinking for over two hours. After getting the horses hitched to the wagon, he went back in. Ma and Aunt Rita had cleaned the kitchen and were sitting in the front room talking.

"It's getting late, Ma, and there is a dark cloud coming from the south."

Ruby glanced at the grandfather clock standing by the front door. "My goodness," she said as she tried to push herself out of the rocker. "We do have to go. I had no idea we'd be here this long."

"Our things are on the table in the breezeway, Zack," said Ruby as Zack pulled his mother to her feet.

As she stood, she bent slightly forward and grabbed her back.

"Are you all right, Ruby?" asked Rita.

"Oh, yes," she answered. "It's just that my back has been hurting real bad today. When I get home I'll rest for a little while and I'll be just fine."

"Get a message to me when you have that little one," said Aunt Rita. "Maybe Injun Billy Joe will stop by to let me know."

"We will, Aunt Rita," assured Zack as he carried the last dishes to the wagon.

"Oh, wait a minute, Ruby. I almost forgot!" said Rita as she ran back into the house. Soon she reappeared with a neat little stack of baby clothes, some crocheted, some made out of beautiful soft pastel material, and some were obviously hand-me-downs. Over her arm was a baby blanket, which Zack figured she had made especially for the new baby. He thought it looked like she had stitched a lot of love into it.

Ruby took time to examine each piece and exclaim over it. "Thank you, Rita, this will help so much." Ruby handed the things to Zack then gave her thoughtful sister a big hug.

Zack helped his mother and siblings into the wagon and started the horses moving. The dark cloud was closer and the wind was really whipping up. Zack slapped the team to a trot, hoping to get home without getting wet.

Before long, a few large drops began to sting their arms and face. "Billy Jake," called Ruby, "dig that old blanket out from under the seat, and y'all cover up. We'll be home soon."

Zack noticed that his mother seemed to be in pain as she spoke.

"Ma, ain't it about time for you to have that baby?" Zack asked.

"I didn't think so, Zack," whispered Ruby biting her lip in pain, "but I'm afraid that whether it's time or not it will be here within the next few hours."

"Ma, I think that as soon as I get you and the young'uns unloaded and the wagon put up, I'd better see if I can get Io's mother to come help." Zack was beginning to feel the frustration of the situation. "She said she wanted to be here and I… I… Ma, I sure don't know nothing about birthin' a baby!"

By the time they pulled up to the house, the wind whipped viciously and the blackened sky was dispensing a torrential downpour.

Chapter Fourteen

The Miracle

Zack saddled Betsy and quickly swung himself up. He urged Betsy into a run toward the Seminole village.

I wish there was a Doctor close, Zack thought, *but I really do trust the Indians. Injun Joe always seems to know what to do and White Fawn offered to help. I know she delivers most of the Indian babies.*

He hurried on. The rain stung his face and his clothes whipped his back. He could barely see ten feet ahead. Small limbs and other debris blew across the already muddy road.

All of a sudden, Betsy shied to one side and reared up. Zack almost hit the muddy road.

"Wha--? Betsy!" he yelled. "What's wrong with you?"

No sooner had he yelled at his faithful horse than he was face to face with an oncoming rider.

"Zack," called Billy Joe. "Where are you going in this awful weather?"

"Oh, Billy Joe," he answered his friend. "Ma is about to have her baby and I was going to get White Fawn to help. What are you doing out here?" He had to yell in order to be heard over the noise of the storm.

"I was coming to check on you," answered Billy Joe. "Go back home, Zack. I'll get White Fawn." With that he spun his big mount back toward the Indian village and Zack quickly rode home. It was much easier riding with the wind and pelting rain to his back. He pulled his jacket collar up to help protect his neck.

As he rode into the back yard, Billy Jake ran out. "I don't think Ma's doin' so good, Zack. I'll take care of Betsy. Maybe you can help Ma."

Before Billy Jake had finished speaking, Zack was through the back door. He ran to his mother's bedroom. She was sitting on the side of her bed.

"Zack, I know you haven't had time to go to the village already," she stated. "Why didn't you go on to get help? I would have been all right until you got back."

Small branches, twigs and leaves assaulted the windows as the wind blasted the house.

"Ma, I no sooner got started than I ran into Injun Billy Joe. He has gone to get Io's mother. I'm sure they'll be here soon."

Zack glanced out the window and realized something had to be done to protect the house and animals.

"Ma," he asked, "will you be all right until I can secure everything around the house? I need to board the windows, and take all the loose stuff to the barn."

"I'm sure I will, Zack. Do what you need to do." Worried, Zack still hovered over her. "Go!" she ordered.

As he rushed through the front room, he noticed JJ and Harmony Belle huddled in a corner, along with Tom and Bubba. Tears flowed down Harmony Belle's face as she tightened her grip on poor Tom. Her big brown eyes stared up at Zack in fear.

Zack knelt and pulled kids and pets close.

"I'm scared, Zack," whimpered Harmony Belle. "Will you stay here with us? Billy Jake said we couldn't go into Ma's room 'cause she's too sick."

"Is Ma goin' to be all right?" asked Jesse Jordan in subdued tones. "She don't sound so good."

"She's going to be just fine, JJ. As soon as this baby gets here, she'll be back to her old self, you'll see."

Zack picked up Harmony Belle, still clutching Tom, and, with his arm around Jesse Jordan's shoulder, he guided them to the sofa.

Bubba followed, wagging his tail appreciatively. He knew he was not usually allowed in the house.

"Sit here, Harmony Belle, and JJ, why don't you light the lamps. It's way too dark in here. I've got to run out and help Billy Jake, and I'll be right back in."

As JJ reached up to the fireplace mantle for the matches, Zack grabbed a dry jacket and hat from the wooden pegs by the back door and ran to the barn.

"Billy Jake," he called. "Are you in here?"

He tried to open the barn door, but the wind jerked it, slamming him and the door back against the barn.

Fighting against the fierce gale, he finally shut and secured the door behind him. "Billy Jake," he called again, unable to see through the darkness. "Are you in here?"

There was no answer. Zack realized that Betsy was not in the barn as he had expected.

He battled his way out of the barn and rushed to the barnyard. "Billy Jake," he shouted again, but there was no answer.

The chickens were huddled in one corner where the fence met the barn. He quickly drove them through the back barn door to the safety of the barn and secured it behind them.

Zack ran around to the side and found Betsy standing over his prostrate brother as if to protect him from the vicious wind and rain. His head and arm was bloody. A dead limb had broken from a nearby tree. Either it had hit Billy Jake from behind, knocking him unconscious, or he was knocked out when his head hit the heavy wooden feeding trough. A tree limb lay across one arm.

"Come on, Betsy," called Zack as he lifted his brother and carried him the short distance to the barn. The horse stayed close until they reached the door.

After trying several times to open the barn door while holding his limp brother on his shoulder, Zack finally succeeded. Before the had a chance to slam shut again, Betsy rushed into the barn, flinging her head up and down and snorting her appreciation.

I sure do wish Injun Billy Joe would hurry, thought Zack as the wind grabbed the wide, hinged closure from him, and again slammed it back against the barn, before crashing shut with a violent jolt. *If I've ever needed help it is now.*

Getting the barn door secured while trying to hold on to Billy Jake seemed almost impossible, but after several attempts, it was closed and locked.

Now, if I can just get Billy Jake into the house, he thought, *maybe I can see how badly he's hurt.*

He battled against pelting rain and wind. *If this is not a hurricane,* he thought, *it is mighty close to it.*

Lightening hit a nearby tree, illuminating the entire area and producing a loud cracking sound. The earth rumbled and shook beneath him.

Zack realized his progress was terribly slow.

His feet splashed in deepening water as he lugged his brother closer to the house. Without warning his right foot sunk into a hole and he went to his knees, dropping Billy Jake into the water.

While attempting to get a better grip on his brother, he prayed, *God please help me get Billy Jake into the house.* With that prayer, he again lifted his unconscious brother and stumbled toward the porch.

Debris and blinding rain flew past them, but finally he reached the steps.

"JJ," he yelled. "JJ, open the door!"

In a moment the door was opened and JJ was asking with a concerned look, "What happened, Zack? What happened to my brother?"

Harmony Belle began wailing and screeching with loud, fearful shrieks.

Upon hearing the commotion, Ruby appeared in the kitchen doorway. "Harmony Belle, what's the matter?"

Harmony Belle was too emotional to answer, move, or hush.

Seeing Zack holding Billy Jake, Ruby quickly led the way toward the living room where Zack placed his brother on the floor.

"Get some water and a washcloth, JJ," she ordered, and then suddenly bent double with another pain.

Zack grabbed her to keep her from falling. "Ma, you can't do this. Here, let me get you back to bed."

The back door opened and there stood Io and her mother, dripping wet.

"Oh, my," exclaimed White Fawn. "You *do* need help! Io, tell Billy Joe to hurry and finish securing those shutters and then come help with Billy Jake. What has happened to him?"

"I'll go, Io. You stay here and help with Ma," said Jesse Jordan as he bolted out the door.

"I think he was either knocked out by a flying branch or just knocked down and maybe hit his head on the pig trough," Zack explained.

"Zack," said White Fawn, taking control, "Let me get Miss Ruby back to bed. Io, do what you can for Billy Jake until your uncle comes in. He'll know what to do for him. Zack, please see what is wrong with Harmony Belle."

Another loud clap of thunder shook the creaking house, followed by a forceful, gust of wind. The whole building seemed to moan.

Realizing Harmony Belle was still screaming, Zack rushed back into the kitchen. His little sister had not moved, nor had she taken her left fingers from her slobbering mouth. Her long curls were soaking wet, clinging to her tear-stained cheeks. The poor cat was still gripped tightly under her right arm and his hind legs hung helplessly, almost reaching the floor.

Zack released Harmony Belle's grip on frightened Tom and he hit the floor. With one long leap he bounded to the corner and began licking his fur.

Zack lifted Harmony Belle to a chair and pulled her hand from her mouth. "Shush-h-h" he consoled. "Why are you crying like that? Shush-h-h."

"Mamma's hurt and crying, an'...an' Billy Jake is dead, an'... the house is going to blow away an'..." she started crying again as Zack wiped her face with a wet towel.

"No, Harmony Belle," he consoled. "Billy Jake is not dead, and Ma's going to be all right. She's having a baby."

"A baby?" asked Harmony Belle between convulsive sobs and sniffs. "How can she do that? Where is she getting a baby?"

"Well, for now, just know that she is going to give us another little brother or sister. And Billy Jake ain't dead. He just got hurt out in the barnyard. Here," he said as he carried her toward the living room, "you can go see Billy Jake for yourself."

Io was kneeling over the injured boy washing his wounds. "He seems to be regaining consciousness," she told Zack.

"Are you all right, Billy Jake?" Io asked as she applied a wet towel to his forehead.

Billy Jake opened his eyes. "Io," he whispered, and he again drifted into sleep. Io continued to wipe his face with a wet towel. Again he opened his eyes.

"Billy Jake," she asked, "where do you hurt?"

"My head… my head hurts, but I think… why am I bloody?" he asked as he stared at his hands.

"You got hurt when you went to put Betsy in the barn," said Zack.

The house again shook, rattling the windows, even though Injun Billy Joe had finished placing the shutters over them. Continuous loud lightening cracks, followed immediately by rolling thunder let them know that the lightening was dangerously close.

Zack gently stood Harmony Belle on the floor. She sat down close to her injured brother and laid her head on his chest. "Does it hurt, Billy Jake?" she asked. "What hurt you?"

"I'm not sure, Harmony Belle," said Billy Jake as Zack examined the back of his head. "I think something hit me from behind. I was going to put Betsy in the barn and that's about all I can remember."

"I guess something did hit you. You have a big knot on the back of your head, but there is this huge lump and open gash on the left side. The best I could tell, you got knocked down and hit your head on the feeding trough."

"Here," said Io, "let me wash it so we can see how bad it is. I didn't realize the back of his head was injured, too."

Zack caught Io's glance and they smiled. "I haven't even had a chance to speak to you, Io," said Zack as he touched her hand.

"It's been pretty chaotic ever since we got here." She smiled.

"Billy Joe must have found something that needed to be done outside," said Zack. "Maybe I should go see if I can help."

"Io," called White Fawn.

As Io got close to her mother, Zack heard her say "She's having a real bad time. The baby is turned sideways, and it seems like the cord is around its neck. I don't know if I can turn it, but I'm going to try. Make sure we have boiling water and ask Zack to get me some scissors."

When Zack heard, he immediately ran to the kitchen and built a fire in the stove and filled the kettle with water. I'm *so glad I have someone to help,* he thought. *I would never have known what to do.*

Injun Billy Joe came in with JJ at his heels. "The wind tore the fence down and the hogs got out, but we finally found them," JJ announced proudly.

"With this weather I'm afraid everything will blow down. I hope it won't get any worse," said Zack. "I really appreciate all the help."

"That is what friends are for, Zack," answered Billy Joe as he washed his hands and face. "How is your mother?"

"I heard White Fawn say she's having a rough time. She said something about the baby being turned sideways, and the cord is around its neck. I'm really worried, Billy Joe. She's too old to have to go through this."

"She will be fine, Zack. White Fawn has brought many babies into this world. She delivers most of the babies born in the village. Miss Ruby will be all right."

They went in to check on Billy Jake. He was propped up on the couch. Harmony Belle had settled into playing with Annie, her rag doll. The cat was nowhere to be seen, but Bubba was asleep at her feet.

JJ put a pillow on the floor and lay down but he raised his head as another blast of wind slammed debris across the porch.

Zack went to the kitchen and got the hot water and scissors, then went to the bedroom where White Fawn and Io were bent over Ruby.

Io looked up and said, "Just put them there on the table, Zack. You really shouldn't be in here."

"Zack ," whispered Ruby as she held her hand out to him. Zack knelt beside his mother. "I don't know if I can do this, but…" Her grip tightened on his hand. Through clenched teeth she tried to muffle a scream. "Zack, I don't think I'm going to make it." Her voice was so weak that Zack could barely hear her.

Zack's thoughts swirled. He tried to imagine life without his mother.

He lightly rubbed her hand. "Ma, you will do it! We are all praying, and you told me that God will never fail us. If that's true, He *will* help you. I believe He will turn the baby so…"

Zack realized that again he was putting his full trust in the Heavenly Father to whom he had so recently given his life. He recognized his own total helplessness.

With great emotion and tears streaming down his cheeks, he blurted, "Ma, if God don't help you… then…then He don't really love us!" His voice softened as he continued, "Ma, He can't let you die." Laying his head on the edge of the bed, he wept.

Outside the storm seemed to be setting in with renewed vengeance, whipping tree limbs and other flying debris against the house. Zack noticed, but at that moment, all he cared about was his mother and the new baby.

White Fawn laid a gentle hand on his back and said, "Zack, you need to go out so we can deliver this baby."

Zack look up at her questioningly.

She shrugged and whispered, "Son, only God knows, but we will do our very best. You have to trust Him."

Slowly Zack laid his mothers hand on the bed. Stepping into the hall he closed the door. He leaned against the wall then slid to the floor. Crouching there, he buried his head in his hands and prayed silently.

God, I'm so sorry that I was feeling angry at you for allowing my mother to go through so much pain. Please take away my bad attitude. I know I have to learn to trust you, even when I can't see your plan. You've helped me when I've asked you to. I've even thought I wanted to preach and tell others about your love. Please don't let me fail you now. I know that the Bible says that all things work together for our good if we love you. God I do love you, but right now I am so scared. Please, God, turn our baby.

Zack cringed as his mother screamed in pain. He continued his silent prayer. *Forgive me for thinking you have to do everything I ask, but if you can see it is for our good, would you just help Ma? Please don't let her and the baby die.*

"Io," White Fawn said, "put your hand right here and push down as hard as you can. I just felt a little movement. I think the baby is turning."

Zack quickly opened the door. Ruby looked so pale that Zack wondered if she were dead.

Suddenly she raised her head from the pillow and with a determined grimace her body began to shake.

"Ruby, the baby just turned! Now push! Push, Ruby, push! You can do it!"

"Zack, bring some more hot water," said White Fawn.

Zack ran from the room with a new assurance that God was in full control and that his mother would be all right.

Injun Billy Joe and Billy Jake looked questioning at Zack as he ran through the front room, toward the kitchen. "I think she's going to be all right," Zack called over his shoulder.

As he hurried back through the living room, Zack said, "White Fawn said the baby just turned." He heard Billy Jake say something but was already too far away to understand.

"Put the pan here, Zack," Io instructed, motioning to a small table. "Thanks," she said, flashing a confident smile. "Now, go keep the men company."

Zack carefully placed the hot water on the table and without a word he slipped his arms around the beautiful Indian girl that he had grown to love so dearly.

Io gave him a fast hug then pushed him toward the door.

As he reached the door, he heard his mother groan. Zack stopped and his hand grasped the door frame.

White Fawn had instructed her to push harder, but then she said, "Miss Ruby, stop pushing. The head is out, but I have to take the cord over the baby's head. The baby's choking and turning purple."

After a moment, White Fawn sighed a sigh that sounded to Zack like a sigh of relief, and then she instructed, "Now push, push hard, Miss Ruby."

Knowing that God and White Fawn had everything under control, Zack left the room.

"Billy Jake," said Billy Joe, "do you want some water, or milk? Are you hungry?"

Zack realized it was very late and no one had eaten supper.

"Harmony Belle, do you want to come help me get supper ready?" Zack asked.

"Take care of her, Bubba," said Harmony Belle as she laid Annie beside the aging dog. Following Zack to the kitchen, she asked, "Why is Ma crying so much? I don't want her to get a baby 'cause it makes her cry."

"Don't worry now, little sister. Ma is goin' to be just fine." He began to set out the left-over food that they had brought back from Aunt Rita's.

"Before you know it you will have a new brother or sister," he told her.

"Where will the baby come from, Zack?"

"Don't worry about that right now. Go tell Injun Billy Joe and JJ to come eat. I'll fix a plate for Billy Jake."

Harmony Belle scurried off and soon returned with JJ. Bubba was right behind them, wagging his whole body in anticipation of a delicious morsel.

"Is Injun Billy Joe comin'?" asked Zack.

"I'm here," said Injun Billy Joe. He stepped into the kitchen with Billy Jake holding onto his arm.

"Are you sure you're able to be up, Billy Jake?"

"He'll be all right," Billy Joe answered for him as he pulled out a chair. "I imagine the biggest problem we'll have is keeping him from eating too much."

By the time they had finished eating, Zack thought the wind might be slowing, even though there was still a torrent of rain.

Zack did not hear a sound coming from his mother's bedroom. He began to worry. Easing down the hall, he slowly opened the bedroom door enough to see White Fawn wrapping a pink blanket around a bundle from which came funny little baby sounds. He bit his lip to try to still the quivering as he watched her lay the newborn close to Ruby.

Oh, God, he thought, *I'm so sorry I ever doubted that you would come through for us.*

Io was tidying the room when she noticed the door had opened. "Come on in and meet your new sister," she whispered with a big smile.

"Ma, are you all right?" Zack knelt beside her.

"I'm real weak and tired, Zack," she murmured, "but I'll be okay."

Gently she pulled the blanket from the baby's face and they both gazed lovingly at this miracle of new life. As he admired his beautiful new sister, instant love for her filled his heart.

"Zack, I have to tell you something that you may find hard to understand. I believe I was dying, but after you had been gone a few minutes, an angel came and stood by me. He placed his hand on my head and said, "*Ruby, God has granted Zack's prayer. You and the baby will live.*" Then he just disappeared and I felt the baby turning inside of me.

Tears of gratitude began to flow down Zack's cheeks as he realized that God had heard him. He bent over for a closer look at his new baby sister and kissed her cheek.

"God is so much better than we can ever know, isn't He, Ma?" he said.

"We couldn't make it without Him, Zack."

Io and White Fawn came closer to get a better look at the new little girl.

"I'm guessing she weighed about six and one-half to seven pounds, don't you, Io?" said White Fawn.

"That is about what I was guessing, Mother," she agreed.

"Ma," Zack smiled with mocked consternation, "what in the world are we gonna do with another young'un?"

Ruby smiled and answered, "We're going to bring the children and Billy Joe in to see her."

Io spoke up, "Mother has already gone to get them."

Soon a small stream of siblings and friends gathered around the bed. Harmony Belle looked around the room. "Zack, I don't see a baby. Where is it?"

Ruby pulled the soft pink blanket from the newborn's face and revealed a squirming, red-faced, black-haired infant. "Meet your new sister, children," she said weakly.

"Sister?" questioned JJ. "I was hoping for a brother. Billy Jake thinks he's too old to play with me any more. I wanted a brother to play with."

"Well, I'm sure you will enjoy this little girl, Jesse Jordan," his mother assured.

JJ stepped close and bent over his new sibling. "Gosh, Ma, why is her face so red?"

"Birthing is very difficult for a baby, JJ," explained Billy Joe. "By tomorrow her red will be gone.

"Billy Jake, how are you feeling?" asked Ruby.

"I'm all right, Ma. It ain't bad at all."

"Ma, can I get you something to eat or drink? I know you must be hungry," said Zack before leaving the room.

"I'll take care of her tonight, Zack," said White Fawn. "You will have your hands full taking care of the rest of the family."

"Zack," said Billy Joe, "I'll help Billy Jake to the bedroom and make sure both boys are tucked in after such a long, traumatic day."

Zack nodded and then sat down in hopes of getting some rest, but Harmony Belle crawled up on his lap. Soon Io sat beside him with a weary sigh.

"Zack, where did Ma get that baby?" asked Harmony Belle.

Zack heard Io snicker as she turned her face away.

Embarrassed, he said, "It's a secret and we'll talk about it later, sweetheart, but for now you have to get ready for bed."

"I want Io to take me to bed," said Harmony Belle.

Io stood and lifted Zack's chubby little sister. "Kiss your brother goodnight," Io suggested. Harmony Belle leaned over and placed a kiss on Zack's cheek.

Zack closed his eyes and propped his head against the wall. Until now, he didn't realize how weary he was.

When Io returned, she sat beside him. A big sigh told Zack that she was also very tired.

"Uncle Billy Joe is taking me home tonight, Zack, but I'll see you in the morning."

"Okay, Io," Zack answered a little surprised. "You will never know how much I–we all appreciate all of you coming."

As Billy Joe returned, Zack and Io stood and walked with him to the back.

Zack offered his hand to his dear friend. "There is no way we could have made it without you. Thanks for being here."

"You're very welcome, Zack," said Billy Joe as he stepped onto the porch. "I'm glad the wind has died down a little." The rain had slowed, but was still a rather nasty downpour.

Just as he finished speaking, a huge gust whipped across them, and a small limb clung to Billy Joe's back.

They laughed as he pulled it from his jacket.

"You spoke too soon, Uncle Billy," said Io. "It isn't finished with us yet."

"From what I can tell in the dark, there'll be a lot of clean-up around here tomorrow," said Zack.

"I have a feeling that the people south and west of here have suffered severe loss," answered Billy Joe. "I'm sure we will be getting bad reports of a brutal hurricane."

Billy Joe then stepped onto the ground. "Oh, look," he said, "the water is half-way up to my knees."

Io stood close to Zack and pulled her shawl tighter around her head and shoulders. "God has blessed us, Zack. Neither my mother nor I thought Miss Ruby was going to be able to have that child. Now, they are both doing well, and Billy Jake will be healed in no time."

"And," she continued mischievously as she carefully walked down the water-logged steps, "another blessing for *me* is that *you*, not *I*, have the very delicate job of explaining to Harmony Belle where her little sister came from." Laughing impishly, she stepped into the debris filled water, and waded to the waiting wagon.

Chapter Fifteen

The Secret

Zack awakened realizing that he had just slept better than he had in weeks.

He lay still, pondering the last few hours. The house was silent except for the rain that still pelted the tin roof and the whine of an occasional gust of wind.

I'm sure that I will have to go to work right away, he thought. *The money Pa left is all but gone.*

He yawned and turned his back to the window, hoping he could go back to sleep.

After a moment, a baby's cry brought him out of the bed.

Ma! He thought, I *wonder how Ma and the baby made it through the night.*

Before his feet could touch the cool floor, he pulled on his socks. As he dressed he wondered what he would cook for breakfast. On the way to the kitchen he stopped to check on his mother and the baby.

Gently, he knocked on her door.

"Come in."

His mother's voice was a little stronger, but he knew it would take a while for her to completely regain her strength.

She was propped up on pillows, nursing the baby. "You're up early," she commented.

"Good morning, Ma," Zack answered. Realizing White Fawn was not there, he questioned, "Where's Io's mother?"

"She said there were a few things she wanted to do. I really don't know what she's doing."

"Do you need me to do anything before I go get breakfast for the young'uns?"

"No, Son," she answered. "I'm doing just fine. I really do appreciate White Fawn staying here all night. She was such a blessing."

"Have you decided on a name for the baby?"

"Not yet," Ma answered, "but I do have some ideas. I'll make a choice soon."

"Are you sure you're all right, Ma? You seem to have somethin' worrin' you."

"I have, Zack," she admitted. "I'm so sorry that we couldn't celebrate your brother's birthday yesterday. This beautiful little girl will have to be his present."

Zack's look of shock brought a gentle laugh to his mother.

"Billy Jake's birthday," said Zack. "Ma, I completely forgot it was his birthday! Oh, but you gave him the best present he could ever ask for. I just realized she was born on his birthday!"

Zack bent over and kissed the tiny little head that was covered with short black hair, and then kissed his mother's forehead.

"Ma, do you think Billy Jake realized it was his birthday yesterday?"

"I really don't know, Son."

"Well, Ma, while you're thinkin' about a good name for my new sister, I'll go see if I can fix some breakfast. The young'uns will be up soon. I don't know how to make biscuits, but I think I can make a hoe-cake."

"Don't worry about it, Zack. You can always feed them corn flakes."

Zack started through the door, and then turned to say, "I think I'll try to do something nice for Billy Jake's birthday today. Do you have any suggestions?"

"Maybe you could get Io to bake a cake. You know chocolate is his favorite. And," she continued, "I have a little gift in my top dresser drawer that you can get out for me."

Zack opened the drawer to find a handsome, red cap and scarf with white stripes on the edges.

"Wow, Ma," said Zack, "when did you crochet these?"

"I've worked on them for several weeks now, just whenever I had a little time."

"They're beautiful. I guess you can give them to him when we have his cake tonight. I'm going to see if I can hustle up some breakfast now."

When Zack reached the front room he smelled an odor like biscuits baking.

In the kitchen White Fawn was almost finished cooking breakfast. Harmony Belle was sitting at the table, waiting.

"Good morning, Zack," greeted White Fawn. "Did you rest well?"

"Yes, Ma'am," he answered. "I was so tired I think I could have rested on a pile of rocks."

Zack noticed that Harmony Belle's hair was not brushed and her untied shoes were on the wrong feet.

"Here, little sister," he said, "let me put your shoes on right and then bring me your hairbrush."

"Miss White Fawn," he continued as Harmony Belle skipped out for her brush, "I didn't expect you to fix breakfast for us. I could have done it, but, of course, it wouldn't have been as good as this."

White Fawn set a bowl on the table. "Are the boys up? It will be ready by the time they get here."

They finished a different but delicious breakfast.

"I'm going out to take care of the stock. Do you need me for anything before I go?"

"No, Zack," answered White Fawn. "There will be much for you to do after that terrible storm last night. Don't worry about anything in here. I plan to stay and help today."

Zack reached for his coat and hat that hung on the wooden pegs behind the door.

"Thank you for all you and your family have done for us, Miss White Fawn. I suspect Ma would be dead right now if..." Zack froze for a moment, biting his lip in deep thought. "...probably," he continued, "the baby, too, if you hadn't been here."

She smiled in acknowledgement as Zack picked up the five-gallon bucket of household scraps that sat by the door.

Zack reached the barn and began throwing hay to the cow, then opened the gate into the pig yard.

"Sooo--kie, Sooo--kie, Sooo--kie", he called loudly. His pig call sounded almost like a loud yodel.

Expecting the big pig to come running, Zack poured the food scraps into the wooden trough. When she didn't come, Zack began checking the split-rail fences. Perhaps the storm had torn a hole somewhere.

As he passed the small pig shelter, he heard a light snorting, followed by heavy breathing. Stepping under the tin-roofed wooden shelter, he saw that Suzie had dug a shallow bed and pushed some of her hay into it. There she lay, obviously in labor.

"Hey, girl," he spoke gently. "Are you all right?"

After checking, he saw she that she had already delivered two piglets.

A bright thought struck him. *This would be a great way to explain to Harmony Belle where her sister came from!*

"You're doing real good, Suzie," he said. "I'll be back in just a couple of minutes." With that he hurried toward the house.

White Fawn and the boys had finished in the kitchen and were probably busy in the other rooms, but there sat Harmony Belle on the kitchen floor, playing with Tom and Annie.

"Hey, sweetheart," Zack said with a smile. "Do you want to go to help me in the barn for a few minutes?"

She jumped up, leaving her faithful cat and rag doll sprawled in the floor, and headed for the door. "Sure, Zack," she grinned. "I like to help feed the horses, and cow, and pigs, and chickens, and all the animals!"

'Wait," ordered Zack as Harmony Belle started to open the door. "It's still sprinkling and you'll need your jacket."

Zack took a jacket and head scarf from the pegs, and put them on his little sister.

"Now we're ready," he said as he took her hand and hurried through the receding water toward the barn. "Do you remember that I said I would tell you a secret?"

"Yes. You said you would tell me where Ma got my sister from."

"That's right, and now I'm going to show you," said Zack.

"Well," said Harmony Belle with a questioning look and outspread hands. "Where did she come from, Zack?"

"Come on, now you can see for yourself where she came from," Zack stated.

Without another word, he led her into the pig yard, and rushed her to the wooden shelter, out of the light rain.

He bent over to talk to her. "Now, Harmony Belle, I'm going to show you exactly where your sister came from."

He turned her around and pointed to the big fat sow that was in the process of birthing her fourth piglet.

"There, now," he said, feeling pleased with himself. "Now you can see where our baby girl came from."

Harmony Belle stared in horror as another tiny piglet shot out from under Suzie's tail and began squealing. Her mouth dropped and tears filled her eyes.

Zack looked with shock at his little sister. She had turned pale and wobbly. They both stood fixed, Zack not knowing what to do, and Harmony Belle trying to launch a terrifying wail from her wide open mouth.

Harmony Belle moved first, yanking away from her confused brother. Before he knew it, she was headed toward the house, screaming, "It's a lie! It's a lie!"

"Wait. Wait!" he commanded. "Let me explain, Harmo…"

She had already reached the door and slammed it behind her.

Zack followed her through the house to his mother's room where Harmony Belle was leaning on the bed, crying as though her heart would break. "It's a lie, it's a lie! I know it's a lie, Ma," she sobbed.

"Sweetheart," Ma was saying. "What's the matter? What's a lie?"

Zack tried to pick her up but she began kicking and crying louder. He put her down, not knowing what to do next.

"Zack," Ma said with great concern. "What has happened?"

As Zack began to explain the problem, an understanding smile crossed his mother's face.

"It's all right, Harmony Belle. She didn't really come from Suzie. Zack was just trying to help you understand how babies are born."

With that, White Fawn, who had been sitting beside the door folding clothes, came and lifted the little girl's tear-streaked face. "Miss Ruby," she offered, "I will handle this if you would like. She will be just fine."

Ma nodded with relief, and kissed her confused daughter. "Go on and play for a while, then you will feel more like visiting with Miss White Fawn so she can make you feel better."

"I don't want to go play. I want her to make me feel better now."

Zack had begun backing into the hall while his little sister continued to look at him with disdain.

He turned around and was face to face with Io. Her mischievous grin told him she had heard everything.

"That went well," she teased, poking him in the ribs.

Without another word Zack left, thinking that from now on he would leave those difficult tasks to the women.

Chapter Sixteen

The Engagement

Two weeks passed. Ruby was feeling much stronger and little *Charity Storm* had become a great joy for the whole family. Zack loved the way she would snuggle against his neck when he held her.

Although Zack and Ruby were very careful in spending the money that he and Pa had brought home from the log camp, Zack knew it would only last another three or four weeks at the most.

Billy Jake had talked about getting a job after school to help, but Zack and Ruby thought it would help more if he took over the responsibility of the farm so Zack could work.

Zack had not been able to sleep very well. He had dreamed or imagined that he heard strange noises that awakened him. Wanting to go back to sleep, he convinced himself that his imagination was playing tricks on him, even though he still seemed to hear muffled growls and squeals. He continued to toss and turn and finally, as the sun began to lighten the eastern horizon, he got up to go feed the animals.

Milk pail in one hand, and the bucket of kitchen scraps in the other, he ambled toward the barn thinking about the noises that had bothered him a couple of hours earlier. In the barn he set down the big bucket of kitchen scraps, hung the milk pail on a nail, then loaded the wheelbarrow with hay. Minnie began walking across the barnyard when she saw him. Her bag was full and she was anxious to be milked.

"Mornin', Minnie," he said cheerfully. "I hope you slept better than I did last night."

Minnie pushed her huge nose into the hay, then while happily chewing she looked at Zack. A few brown blades of hay escaped from her mouth letting the breeze take them.

"I'll take that look as a *thank you*," laughed Zack as he reached for the three-legged milking stool. He set the tin pail on the ground and soon there was a rhythmic whoosh-whoosh of milk as it hit the side of the pail. Before long the pail was full and Minnie was again comfortable. Zack put her back into the pasture and pointed the wheelbarrow toward the horses.

After feed and a few loving pats for his beloved Betsy, Zack went back to the barn and picked up the bucket of slop for Suzie. Her seven piglets were two weeks old now and very active. Zack thought that in a few months, they would be able to sell three or four of them. That should help with some of their expenses.

He poured the scraps into the trough but Suzie did not come. He called and then went into the pen. The fence on the back side had been torn down. His heart jumped and his mouth dropped as he saw mammoth bear tracks. They explained the strange noises he had heard few hours earlier.

Zack soon found the partially eaten carcass of one piglet behind the watering tub. He hurriedly searched for Suzie but she was nowhere to be found. Instead, he found large drag marks leading to the demolished fence and on across the glade toward the swamp. Realizing the size of a bear that could drag a sow as big as Suzie, his heart sank. *What if I had come out to check on the noises I heard during the night?*

Hurriedly he looked for the other pigs and found five of them huddled fearfully in a fence-row thicket. He propped the back barn door open, and drove the scared little pigs into the barn until he could get the fence mended. He then ran to the house to wake Billy Jake. Ma was in the kitchen and as he opened the door he heard her singing while stirring the egg-gravy.

"Ma," Zack knew he sounded stressed.

Ruby wheeled around with a questioning look on her face. "What's wrong, Zack?"

"Ma, that blamed ol' bear has got Suzie and killed and eat one of her babies."

"My Lord, have mercy," exclaimed Ruby. "Are you sure, Zack?"

"I'm sure, Ma. He tore down the fence and you can see the drag marks in the dirt and grass where he drug that big ol' sow toward the swamp."

Just then Billy Jake came in, his mouth wide open in a big yawn. "What about the swamp, Zack?" he asked nonchalantly as he pulled out a chair and sat down, scratching his belly.

"Billy Jake, I have bad news." Zack thought he would rather take a beating than to tell his brother that Suzie was gone.

Billy Jake cocked his head and looked quizzically at his big brother.

"That doggone bear came in last night and ate one of the piglets, then carried Suzie off to the swamp."

Billy Jake stood so fast that his chair tipped onto the floor. "No!" he shouted. "How could that happen? How do you know it was a bear? Maybe she just rooted out under the fence and..."

Zack put his hand on his brother's shoulder. "Billy Jake, I know how much you loved her, but she is gone. The fence was not dug under, it was ripped through and then wallowed down."

By the time he was finished speaking, Billy Jake was off the back porch, totally ignoring the steps.

"I'd better go with him, Ma. Then I'm going to find Injun Billy Joe."

"I expect you both back for breakfast in ten minutes, Zack"

"We'll be back, Ma."

Zack ran to the pigpen where Billy Jake was examining the paw-prints in the damp dirt. Tears streamed down his face as he realized his beloved Suzie was gone.

"I ain't never seen such big footprints before, Zack. Look how deep those tracks are. He must 'ave weighed five hundred pounds or more!"

"I have no idea how much he weighed, Billy Jake," said Zack, "but I do know he must be the biggest one I've ever seen."

They walked around, looking at the signs of struggle, and then Billy Jake saw the remains of the partially eaten piglet. Quickly he grabbed a shovel that was leaning against the barn. Choosing a grassy spot just outside the fence he dug a grave for the meager remains.

"Let's go through the barn," suggested Zack. "That's where I put the other babies."

The five piglets were scurrying around in the hay.

"Do you think they will be old enough to eat, Zack, or do you think they'll have to be fed?"

"We can try giving them milk but we might have to get a bottle for them. Right now we have to get in for breakfast or Ma's gonna' skin us."

As they walked to the house, Billy Jake asked, "Zack, if you go after that bear can I go with you?"

"Ma will have to answer that for you, but I really doubt it. I'm going to see Injun Billy Joe as soon as we finish breakfast, and while I'm gone, you need to see if you can get the pigs to drink milk."

JJ and Harmony Belle were sitting at the table when they came in. There were a lot of questions and conversation about the bear, and Zack let Billy Jake answer them.

Zack's thoughts were on going after that hateful critter.

After breakfast Zack saddled Betsy and turned her toward the Seminole Village.

Injun Billy Joe met him at the door. "Good morning, Zack," greeted Billy Joe. "What brings you here so early?"

"Howdy, Billy Joe," answered Zack as he swung off Betsy and stood beside his friend. "That thieving bear got Billy Jake's sow and one of her babies last night, Billy Joe. Something's got to be done."

"I'm very sorry to hear that, Zack," answered Billy Joe. "He's getting much too bold. Last week he tore into Mister Watkins's barn and took a three-day-old calf."

"I hadn't heard about that," answered Zack. "I reckon the next thing you know he'll have some farmer's young'un."

Billy Joe thought for a moment, and then said, "Mister Watkins and some of the other men have been talking about going after him. I believe it is time for more than talk."

"I'll be ready as soon as we can get some men together," offered Zack.

Billy Joe looked at him quizzically. "How do you think Miss Ruby will feel about your going on a dangerous bear hunt?"

"Well," Zack stopped and scratched his head. "Well, I reckon she might rather I didn't go, but I reckon that wouldn't matter too much. I plan to be in on that hunt."

Just then Io stepped out of her uncle's door. "Well, Zack, would it matter if *I* didn't want you to go?"

Her black hair bounced on her turquoise blouse as she spoke. The rows of bright red, yellow and turquoise decorating the bottom of her full skirt flounced from side to side as she sashayed out to see him.

Zack stuttered something about not knowing she was there, and then got his wits together.

"Hello, Io. I'm pleased to see you."

"Zachariah Bentley," she said with pretended sternness. "You haven't answered my question."

"Well now, Io, are you saying you *don't* want me to go?"

"I think I will go in and let you two talk this out," said Billy Joe with a big smile.

"I have to hurry back soon, but maybe we can take a few minutes for a walk." Zack threw Betsy's reins over a fence, and with his arm around Io's shoulders, they walked to a small stand of palms.

"I'm really sorry about Billy Jake's pig. He was so fond of her, and he was very proud of her litter."

"Yeah," answered Zack. "Io, you should have seen those bear tracks. They was...I mean were the biggest I've ever seen. I just hope we won't have any trouble finding him. He could give us a big fight."

"Zack, please be careful. I know you have to go on the hunt, but I want you to promise me you will be very careful."

"I'll be careful, Io."

They sat in the spotty shade of a palm, holding hands. Zack noticed the sunlight and shadows playing on Io's lovely face as the breeze gently moved the palm fronds.

He talked about Charity Storm and all the ways she was changing and growing. They discussed Billy Jake's injuries and laughed about his surprise when they gave him his birthday cake and gift. They talked about Ruby and how Zack thought she was regaining her strength, although very slowly.

"Zack, she was a little older than most mothers are. I would think that could have a lot to do with it."

"Probably," Zack agreed. "I'm just glad that Pa's not around so she won't ever go through that again."

"You don't talk about him very much, Zack. Do you miss him?"

Zack fell silent for a minute, then said, "Don't reckon I do. I don't really miss him. I think about him sometimes, but when he was drinking, he was so wicked and mean that nobody could stand him. He would go through the house, breaking things and cussin'. The worst part is that if I hadn't given my heart to Jesus, I would probably be just as bad as he was."

"You're a good man, Zack," said Io, "but I'm very glad you gave your heart to God. You have grown so much in a spiritual way. I am very proud of you."

Zack drew her to him in a tight hug, and for a moment he felt like he was not touching the ground.

"Well," said Io as she gently drew away from him, "Go on, Zack. I really want to know more about you and all your family."

Zack let his head lean back against the rough, spiny palm trunk and thought before continuing.

"Many times, when we were smaller, Pa would come in drunk and beat Ma around and take his belt to the young'uns for no good reason. He almost always left them bleeding, and it seemed like if he beat one, he beat them all. He would never let Ma come take care of them, but after we were in bed and I heard him snoring, I'd take some salve and put it on their cuts. Many times I would hold them to try to stop their trembling so they could go to sleep."

"You keep saying *them* and *their*. Did he ever beat you like that?"

"Almost always," Zack admitted. "I reckon I usually got it worse than the others, but I figured I was older and could take it better than they could."

Zack sat for a few moments without speaking as feeling anger stir within him, then he said, "I really don't like to talk about it. It brings back a lot of hatred. I'd rather talk about us."

"About us? What about us?" she asked with pretended innocence.

"Just a minute ago you said you were proud of me. Is that true, Io?"

"Of course it is, Zack."

"Is there more to your feelings than being proud of me?"

"Oh, Zack, I care very deeply for you. In fact I'm in love with you." She grasped his face with both hands and gently kissed his lips.

After a moment Zack took a deep breath and said, "Io, I truly do love you, too. You're constantly on my mind. I can't even imagine life without you. I guess what I'm really saying is, Io, will you marry me?"

Io looked at him with surprise. "Do you really mean that, Zack? Please don't tease me."

"I would never tease you, Io. I love you too much to tease. I know it will be a while before you get your teaching certificate, but if I could just know you plan to be my wife some day, I would be a happy man."

"Yes, Zack," she said. "I would be very proud to know we will someday be married." Io caught a deep breath and smiled a very big smile. "Right now I am so happy I feel like singing."

Their lips met in a kiss that he had dreamed of many times, but *this* kiss far exceeded his very vivid imagination. Zack knew that this was a kiss he would never forget.

He held her tightly for another moment, feeling his passionate body tremble as his arms drew her even closer. "I want this moment to last forever, sweetheart."

Again, his quivering lips sought hers. Her arms tightened around him as she laid her head back in total surrender to his feverish kisses.

"Zack," she whispered, almost inaudibly. "I have longed for this moment for so long!"

Zack wondered if he could possibly be dreaming. *If I am,* he thought, *I hope I never wake up.*

Io relaxed her arms and allowed her head to rest on his pounding chest.

Time stood still for two motionless lovers as they promised lifelong devotion.

For the next hour, they chatted about their future, found silly little things to laugh about and breathlessly embraced each other. Io talked about her family and early years growing up without her dad, who had died when she was six years old.

Zack knew he had much to do, but pulling away from Io was the most difficult.

"I really hate to, sweetheart, but I have to go."

Reluctantly, Io smiled and nodded in agreement, saying she also had some things that she had promised to do for her uncle Billy Joe.

Zack stood and pulled Io to her feet. After a lengthy goodbye kiss, they walked silently back to Billy Joe's house, hand in hand.

Zack took the reins and swung onto Betsy. Io came close and took Zack's hand and said tenderly, "I love you, Zachariah Bentley."

"Io," Zack said, aware of the warmth of her body as she leaned against his leg. "You have made me the happiest man in the world."

He bent over and kissed her upturned forehead, and then started Betsy in a slow trot. He rode a few yards then dug his heels into her sides. She broke into a hard run, as though she were trying to out-run the beat of Zack's happy heart.

Zack stood in the stirrups, and throwing one hand high in the air he hollered a very loud "Whooopeee".

Chapter Seventeen

The Bear Hunt

Zack sat in a chair and leaned back against the wall.

His thoughts were mostly on his time with Io that morning. *When should he tell Ma about his engagement? How would she react? Would Ma and Billy Jake and Jesse Jordan be able to keep the homestead running after he and Io were married?*

He was also enjoying watching Harmony Belle, who seemed to be growing up right before his eyes. He thought she was cute as she pretended to be grown playing with Annie, her worn out doll.

Harmony Belle answered a knock at the back door. Her rag doll dangled from her arm, and as usual, long, wispy curls hung around her chubby face.

"Oh, hello, Mister Injun Billy Joe, please come in," invited Harmony Belle.

Zack and Billy Joe nodded at each other as his friend walked in.

"Well," laughed Billy Joe, "what is all this? You are very grownup today Miss Harmony Belle."

"I am the mother and my baby Annie has been crying. I think her stomach is hurting."

"You know," answered Billy Joe, "it might be her stomach, but I think I might have just the right medicine for her and her mommy."

"You do?" queried the child with anticipation.

"I think I just might." He reached inside his vest and brought out two sticks of mint candy. As he handed them to Harmony Belle he said, "I'm sure you already know this, but mint is very good for a stomach ache."

Harmony Belle thought for a moment and then asked, "Can I give one to Charity Storm? Ma said she has a tummy ache."

"Well, I really don't think this is the right medicine for a baby that young. Maybe we had better let your mother take care of her," answered Billy Joe.

"Okay, thank you, Injun Billy Joe." She giggled as she dragged Annie by one leg to the front room to enjoy the medicine.

Ruby brought Charity Storm into the kitchen. "It's been a while since you saw Charity, Billy Joe. Can you tell she's grown any?"

"Yes, Miss Ruby, and she is a beautiful baby, too. She looks a lot like her mother with her dark hair. I understand her stomach has not been well."

"She has been having a little colic at night, but she rested better last night. I guess I'll have to be more careful what I eat," smiled Ruby

"What brings you here, Billy Joe?" asked Zack. He knew Billy Joe only stopped by when he had a purpose.

"I have spent most of the day getting volunteers ready for the hunt. Randall Watkins, Lee Roy Larson and his oldest son, Phillip, said they will be ready by first light in the morning. Randall has those two red bloodhounds, and he plans to bring them."

"I've heard they are the best in this area," answered Zack. "They tell me that them hounds will track and fight anything that walks in them woods. I reckon I need to get a good night of sleep tonight."

"Zack, maybe you should let the older men do the bear hunting," objected Ruby. "You don't have any experience at that sort of thing."

"Ma," explained Zack, "that rascal took Billy Jake's pet sow and one of her babies. It is my responsibility to go after him."

Zack pushed his chair up and went to his mother's side. "Ma, you keep forgetting I'm grown. I promise I'll be very careful."

Ruby stared at her oldest son and then smiled and handed the baby to him. "Here, hold your little sister while I get supper ready."

"Billy Joe, will you have supper with us?" she asked.

"Thank you, Miss Ruby, but I need to get home. I've been gone most of the day and I have a lot to do to get ready for tomorrow."

"Well, I hope we can finally get that bear," said Zack.

Billy Jake walked into the kitchen.

Zack continued. "How many times over the past ten years has a posse gone after him and come back with nothing?"

"I'm not sure how many times, probably six or seven, but I remember about four years ago a group went into the Everglades and the bear found them. He nearly killed Mister Parton's son, but they didn't even get a shot off at the bear. He disappeared back into the brush before they knew what had happened."

Ruby stopped and turned toward the men. "That's why I don't think y'all should go. I'll be worried to death 'til you get home."

"I want to go, Zack," said Billy Jake. "After all, it was my sow and pig he took."

"Merciful Lord, boy," exclaimed Ruby. "You are much too young. I don't even want Zack to go but I reckon he's bound and determined."

Billy Jake sat down, crossed his arms, and displayed a pouting frown.

"Billy Jake," said Zack, "you are the only one Ma can depend on to help her and to make sure the young'uns do their chores. I don't blame you for wanting to go, but we really need you here tomorrow. By the way, were you able to get the piglets to drink milk from the pan?"

At first Billy Jake did not answer, but then he said, "They were real messy but I think they'll get the hang of it pretty fast." His frown relaxed enough to let Zack know he would be all right.

Ruby smiled her appreciation for Billy Jake's help. "I really will need you here, son."

"Ma," said Zack, picking up from where he was before Billy Jake came in, "we'll be very careful, I promise."

Billy Joe started to leave, then said, "The men are meeting at my house since it's closest to the 'Glades. I'll see you at sun-up."

"I'll be there," answered Zack.

The next morning Zack saddled Betsy and arrived at Billy Joe's house before the sun was up. Mister Watkins and his bloodhounds were already there.

Billy Joe had hot herbal tea ready for the men. "Come in and have some tea while we wait for the Larsons."

Zack welcomed the hot liquid. "I packed quite a bit of food for the trip. Ma cooked some salt pork and biscuits. I think there's enough for everybody."

"Once them hounds get a scent of that bear," said Mister Watkins, "we probably won't be slowing down to eat. You'll have to eat on the run, son."

For the next few minutes Zack sipped his tea and listened to the other men talk about the damage the bear had recently caused and where the best place to find his trail would be. He was feeling a little anxiety and for a fleeting moment he wished he had a bottle of whisky to steady his nerves. Immediately, he was ashamed and hoped that he would never think about drinking again, but he figured that his anxiety was normal.

Zack thought about each of the other four men who would be with him and came to the conclusion that he could not be with a better group. They were all Christians so none drank. This was good because, since becoming a Christian, he had not really been tested by being with a group that was drinking. Was his salvation established enough to deal with strong temptation? Was he really able to accept God's grace as sufficient?

He was also glad that Phillip was coming. Phil was two years older than Zack, but they had become good friends right after Zack gave his life to God.

"Here they are," said Billy Joe as the sound of hoofs approached. "They need to come in and drink some tea. It will give extra strength and endurance for the day."

After greetings the men finished their tea and put the horses out to pasture.

"We'll be on foot, so everyone take extra care to stay close to the group," instructed Mister Watkins. "If you get separated, you'll be on your own in them 'Glades, an' that ain't no good place to be all by yourself."

Mister Watkins and his dogs took the lead. Billy Joe and Lee Roy Larson followed next, hacking a trail when needed. Phil and Zack followed behind them.

Zack had spent a lot of time last night cleaning and checking out the 30-30 Winchester that had belonged to his father. It was a single shot, but if he aimed well, it would do the job. Each man seemed satisfied with the weapon he had chosen, and Zack certainly had plenty of ammunition.

Before long they found deep bear tracks leading through a muddy bottom.

"Whoa, Red," called Mister Watkins as he pulled the big dogs to a stop. "I'm glad they weren't on a real hot trail yet, or those big dogs would be draggin' me."

They laughed.

"I can see him now," laughed Phil, "going through brush and slough, trying to hang onto those two monstrous red hounds."

"Yeah," answered Zack, "I'm wondering how he will handle them when they take a good hot scent."

"We'll see," said Phil.

"Would you look at them tracks," said Lee Roy. "I never seen a bear track that big before."

"And look how deep it is," said Billy Joe. "Judging by this track he must be larger than any bear I've ever seen."

"I just hope he won't go back to the homestead tonight while we're out here looking for him," said Phil.

"That's doubtful," answered Billy Joe, "since he got that big hog night before last. That will probably keep him a few more days."

"Those tracks lead south toward the big swamp," said Mister Watkins. "Come here Red," he said, directing the dogs to sniff the paw prints.

After a few sniffs, the big red dogs began to run around, almost in circles, with their noses on the ground, happily wagging their tails.

Before anyone knew what they were doing, they broke into a dead run straight south, with noses to the ground. The sound of their bays, yelps and yaps was almost ear-piercing. At first it looked like their take-off took Mister Watkins by surprise. As they jerked his arm straight, he had to work hard to keep them from dragging him but he quickly recovered control amid the other men's hardy laughs.

"Here, let me take one of them," offered Lee Roy. "The two of them are too much for one man."

Mister Watkins gladly handed one leash to Lee Roy. "That feels better already," he yelled over the wails and howls.

They trotted when the glades were smooth enough, but were slowed to a walk when the palmettos and brush were thick. After following the dogs for almost five hours, Zack thought his legs were too tired to keep going.

"It's almost noon," said Lee Roy. "Let's stop here for a quick bite."

They had come to a small clearing where the sun was shining and the grass was only knee-high. Each man laid out his food to share with the others.

Zack didn't realize how thirsty he was until he let a few mouthfuls of water cool his throat.

They ate a fairly small meal as they knew they couldn't keep up with the dogs if they were too full.

After resting for a few minutes, Billy Joe said, "If we plan to get a bear, we had better be off."

While they were packing their back packs, Billy Joe continued, "For many years now I've been all over these swamps, and from the direction the dogs are leading, I think I know where that bear is living."

"Sure 'nuf, Billy Joe?" questioned Phil. "Is it close?"

"If they're leading to where I think they are, we should make it in another four or five hours. Those paw prints have not varied at all.

They still are headed due south. There is a huge mound in a clearing, and there is a cave in the mound. A foot or maybe two feet of water surrounds the entire mound. "

"You've seen it before?" asked Mr. Watkins.

"Yes, several times," answered Billy Joe. "When I was a young boy my father took me all over these swamps and woods. We spent many days hunting and gathering special herbs. I am well acquainted with all the Everglades.

"How big is the mound?" asked Phil.

Well, my guess is that it stands about twelve feet above the water and is probably thirty feet wide and fifty feet long.

"What do you think made a mound like that?" asked Zack. "Could it be an old Indian burial ground?"

"No, it is definitely not a burial ground. That mound was here long before the Indians were pushed into the Everglades. All the Indians think it is a home of the gods."

"Are you superstitious, Billy Joe?" asked Lee Roy.

"Not at all," answered the Indian. "I believe in one God."

"I guess we all do," said Mister Watkins, "and right now I feel a need for us to ask him to be with us on this hunt."

"I agree," said Phil.

They bowed their heads and Mister Watkins prayed for guidance, strength and wisdom for this hunt. He then untied the hounds and handed one leash to Zack while he took the lead with the biggest hound. Billy Joe continued to slash a trail where needed. After a few minutes of fast trotting, Zack wondered how his friend had controlled those muscular animals for so long. His arm was already getting sore. They continued through woods and glades, and at times swampy areas. Although the water came to their ankles or knees, it didn't slow them. They traveled another three and one half hours before they came to another small clearing. Billy Joe squatted down to examine the grass that had been trampled by the bear. It was just beginning to straighten so he knew that the bear had been there within the past hour.

"He's not too far ahead," he announced.

They passed through a little clump of bushes into a small open space about two hundred yards wide. The bear had run straight through the open clearing. From past experience, the older men knew the bear was aware that they were chasing him.

"He knows we're on his trail," said Lee Roy, "and he's making good time."

"He is headed for home," added Billy Joe. "That means we have to be ready to swim through very deep water, circle cypress trees and cut through some of the thickest palmettos you have ever seen."

"If he reaches the big swamp before we get him, he will be hard to follow," said Zack. "I hope we don't lose him."

"These hounds ain't about to lose his trail, Son," assured Mister Watkins.

"I'm sure in my heart that I know exactly where he's headed," answered Billy Joe. "He's headed for that mound, and is running faster now. Just look how far apart his tracks are."

"As long as he's going in a straight line," said Lee Roy, "we know he's not doubling back on us like he did to Paul Parton four years ago."

Zack felt a shiver run down his spine as he thought about the danger they could be facing.

Billy Joe noticed that Zack kept looking behind them. "Do you think he's behind us, Zack?"

"No, but I hate surprises," Zack answered.

They were now through the clearing and suddenly found themselves in some thick brush. The bear had not gone around any thicket, but had gone through them, breaking down brush and small trees like match-sticks. They proceeded as slowly as the dogs would allow, keeping a close watch all around.

After another half hour, they left the 'Glades and found themselves in the big swamp. In most places the water was deep and they swam with one hand while keeping their weapons dry. Zack knew that there were dangerous snakes in this dark water. Vines and brush were so thick in other places that they could hardly cut through. The thick canopy of trees made it seem almost like night.

They had seen several alligators, and Zack knew from experience that for every one they saw, there were many more that they didn't see. Neither Zack nor Phil had ever been in the big swamp before, but Zack was no stranger to swamps. He could vividly remember sawing mammoth cypress with his pa in water up to his armpits. Alligators and snakes were all around then, too, but he dared not let his pa know he was scared.

"I'm not the bravest man in the world, even in the daylight," said Lee Roy, "but here in this dark swamp filled with 'gators, snakes, and bears I'm plumb scared."

"You ain't the only one," admitted Mr. Watkins. "I'm scared, too."

"Are you scared, Billy Joe?" asked Phil.

Billy Joe answered with a smile, which could have meant yes or no.

"Billy Joe," said Lee Roy, "I bet you are just as scared as we are."

After a few more minutes, Billy Joe stopped and pointed his gun south. "The bear cave is close now. Go slowly, and keep your guns ready to fire."

After they had walked another five or ten minutes, the mound came into view.

"It looks just like Injun Billy Joe described it," said Zack.

When they were at the water's edge, they tied the hounds to a large tree, but Mister Watkins made sure that the biggest hound could be turned loose with just a single yank on his leash.

A heavy silence hung over the swamp like a blanket. No birds were singing, no squirrels were barking, and there was no sound of fish jumping although they knew that these waters were teeming with them. The only sound was the baying of the hounds.

"The animals are all quiet because the bear just came through here," said Billy Joe. Then he smiled and teased, "They are all afraid like the white man."

The men returned the good-hearted tease with a smile.

"What should we do now, Billy Joe?" asked Phil.

"We need to gather a lot of dry sticks, wood and Spanish moss, to build a fire that will produce a lot of smoke at the mouth of the cave. When the bear comes out, we'll shoot him."

"That sounds good to me, except that I ain't too crazy about the mouth of the cave thing," commented Mister Watkins. "Bears can run awful fast."

"Yeah," said Lee Roy, "but we'll all have our guns aimed and ready."

The men set about gathering the materials needed.

Billy Joe and Lee Roy then went to the left side of the opening where a good flow of air would draw the smoke into the cave. Quickly they started the fire then put a mammoth mound of moss on the flame. The other men stood guard with guns ready.

It only took about five minutes for the moss to create a heavy black smoke. It began to slowly drift into the cave.

Zack, Phil and Mister Watkins stood back about fifteen to twenty feet, ready for action. Lee Roy and Billy Joe eased backward a few feet from the fire.

After about ten minutes Phil said, "It don't look like he's coming out. Do you reckon there's another exit somewhere?"

"No," answered Billy Joe. "This is the only one. It won't be long now."

Within another minute they heard an angry growl coming from the mound. Zack's heart began to beat so hard that he was afraid the other men might hear it. He double checked his gun to be sure it was ready to fire.

Billy Joe and Lee Roy were directly in front of the mouth of the cave with guns poised for action, but Lee Roy was a few feet closer than Billy Joe. Zack, Mister Watkins and Phil spread out to get a clear shot when the beast showed himself.

"There're two of them," yelled Billy Joe as they heard the reverberation of two loud, angry growls mixing together.

The growls were now a constant roar of defiance and anger. Zack believed he could feel the very ground shaking where he stood. When added to the baying and barks of the two hounds, the noise was mind-boggling.

The growls seemed to be sounds of hatred for the man-creatures that had chased him and caused the smoke to infiltrate their cave.

Without warning one huge bear came bounding out of the cave. The other was no more than eight or ten feet behind him. Zack had never seen such speed in an animal that enormous. Before he could pull the trigger, the first bear had almost reached Lee Roy and Billy Joe.

Mister Watkins quickly jerked loose the leash that restrained Big Red, and then, five weapons fired, but they each fired at the same bear, who fell dead about six feet from Lee Roy.

The second bear was now on her hind legs, towering above Lee Roy. Her lip curled upward displaying mammoth fangs. Her mouth was wide open in an earsplitting growl.

The men were furiously trying to reload their weapons as the she-bear reached Lee Roy. Knowing he did not have enough time to reload, he clubbed his rifle and struck a blow to the bear's head. This only seemed to enrage her more as she swung her massive head from side to side while emitting vicious guttural noises. She reached out with her mighty front paw, knocking Lee Roy to the ground while severely slashing his forearm in the process. His rifle landed in the water, out of his reach.

Just as the bear turned to attack Lee Roy again, Big Red hurled himself through the air and fastened his teeth into the bear's neck. Bear and dog fell to the ground beside Lee Roy who was desperately trying to scramble to safety. The bear gave Lee Roy another nasty rake with her razor-like claws, leaving four long gashes across his shoulder.

Forced to give her attention to the tenacious hound that was holding onto her neck with a death grip, the bear tried to pull him off. She gave him a vicious rake with her paw but he was squirming too much for her to do severe damage.

The other hound was pulling hard, trying to find a way to get loose and join the fracas.

While the men, who had now reloaded their weapons, were trying to get into position to shoot the bear without hitting the dog, Billy Joe calmly walked over to the bear and pulled the trigger.

Blood poured from a big hole that appeared in her side. She tried to reach Billy Joe with her deadly claws but the Indian had deftly backed away to reload.

Zack got off a shot that hit her in the small of the back, breaking it. The tenacious hound still gripped the neck of the bear, and would not let go until Mister Watkins grabbed him by the scruff of the neck and pulled him off. He then ended the fight by putting a bullet into the bear's head.

Lee Roy had crawled a few feet away from imminent danger. Phil and Zack were quickly beside him examining his wounds. There were serious gashes on his arm and back, three of which went to the bone. Blood poured from each of them, turning the shallow water red where he lay.

Mister Watkins built a small fire close to where the dogs were tied, and then went to see if he could help Lee Roy.

"Pa," said Phil as he helped his father to a more comfortable spot, "we really have to give God the praise that you're not dead."

"That's for sure," added Zack. "I believe God heard our prayer for safety this morning and I'm glad that we're all alive, but I wish no one had been hurt."

"I've served him now, goin' on forty years, and he ain't never failed me yet. I've seen some rough times, but I always got through them," said Mister Watkins, "and we'll get through this, too."

Billy Joe disappeared into the swamp and soon returned with a handful of leaves.

"Big Red is a very good hound," said Billy Joe as he joined the other men. "It looks like he has some minor gashes, too. There may be one wound that needs attention, but he was able to stay away from the bear's claws pretty well."

As he spoke, Billy Joe heated the leaves over the fire until they were soft and pliable, and then tied them on Lee Roy's wounds with pieces of the shirt that the bear had shredded.

"These leaves will help you heal quickly," said Billy Joe.

The men decided that since Lee Roy was weakened by the loss of so much blood they would spend the night in the cave. Billy Joe took a burning piece of dried cypress and explored the cavern.

He came out and said, "It's dry and comfortable in there. It will be a good place to spend the night."

Zack and Phil skinned the mammoth animals and cut up some meat for the hounds, but not knowing how fast Lee Roy could travel, they decided they could not carry any meat home. It might be spoiled before they could get it there, but they cooked enough to eat on the way back.

Sitting around the campfire, the hunters enjoyed bear steak for supper. They ate slowly while reliving every detail of the hunt and the awesome battle with the bears.

Zack and Phil cleaned and scraped the bearskins as well as possible and then tightly rolled and tied them for the trek home tomorrow. Billy Joe said he would see to it that they were properly tanned when they got back.

Except for Lee Roy awaking in pain several times, the men slept well that night. They took turns guarding the entrance, just in case another bear might come by. Except for an occasional small animal and two deer, everything was calm.

It had taken only one day to reach the mound, but due to Lee Roy's condition, they were forced to make camp the next afternoon after getting through the big swamp.

Lee Roy's fever had shot high and he was delirious. He had also become sick to his stomach. Again, Billy Joe gathered leaves and roots from the woods and swamp. He used the roots to brew a drink for Lee Roy, and the leaves to treat his wounds. He changed the bandages, using the fresh leaves that he had just gathered and heated. By the time he was finished, Lee Roy was becoming sleepy. Soon he was fast asleep.

The other men sat around the campfire discussing the events of the past two days before finding their own places to sleep.

As they retired, Billy Joe said, "I don't want anyone to wake Lee Roy in the morning. We'll leave when he wakes up on his own, and that may be mid-morning."

"Billy Joe," said Phil, "where did you learn about all those roots and leaves that's good for medicine?"

"It is passed from one generation to the next. My grandfather was a very wise medicine man and he taught my father. I've had more training than most. My father was the best ever at curing infections, fever, and even blood poison."

They took their time the next morning getting up and preparing the breakfast. Finally, Lee Roy opened his eyes and realized it was late.

"Why didn't someone call me?" he asked.

"Billy Joe said you should be allowed to sleep until you woke up on your own," Phil explained.

"Billy Joe," Lee Roy asked, "what was that awful tasting stuff you made me drink last night?"

"Good medicine," laughed Billy Joe. "You slept well, and I assume you feel better this morning, right?"

"I do feel pretty good considering how bad I felt last night, but I am still in a lot of pain."

"Changing the subject," said Mister Watson, "since Lee Roy did battle with that bear, I think he should take one of the skins home."

"That sounds good to me," said Phil. "And since it was Billy Jake's pet sow that got killed, I think Zack should take the other one to him."

The men were all in agreement, and Zack was proud to be able to give the skin to Billy Jake.

They reached Billy Joe's house by late afternoon.

Chapter Eighteen

Revealing Decisions

The fall had almost passed, and cold weather came in a little earlier than usual. Zack and Billy Jake had plowed a large area to put in the fall garden. They planted turnips, collards, peas, and beans. They had also planted velvet beans to help feed the cows, horses and mule. All the crops were looking good. Late fall had been a very busy time for the Bentleys.

"I hope this cold weather won't get our garden," said Zack as he hung his jacket behind the door. "I ain't used to havin' to worry about losing our winter crops to frost. It's been a couple of years since we had a freeze, and that was just one morning."

"Maybe it'll warm up after these two freezing mornings," answered Ruby. "About every five years or so, we'll get a night or two of cold weather. I have a feeling we've seen the last frost for this year."

"All the plants that are up looked real good to me," said Billy Jake. "The greens are getting pretty big, and they looked all right this morning. If everything in that garden makes good this winter, we'll have a lot of canning to do, but at least we won't go hungry for a while."

"With everything happening this past summer, I wasn't able to do much with our spring garden," said Ruby. "We made enough to keep us going, but I didn't do much canning."

"Ma, you made some of the best bread 'n' butter pickles I've ever tasted," said JJ.

"Well, the cucumbers did real good this summer," agreed Ma.

"Ma," said Zack thoughtfully, "I've been thinkin' about going into town to see Mr. O'Bannon about a job on his boat. With the crops in the ground, I think Billy Jake and JJ can keep it weeded for a while and harvest it when it's ready."

Zack sat quietly, waiting for his mother's answer.

They had spent almost all they had left to buy a good plow mule, and she made the work much easier and faster for the boys to plant the garden. Zack felt she was well worth the money they had spent. The mule was a help with several heavy jobs around the farm, but he also knew their money was all but gone.

Finally Ruby said, "How long will you have to be gone on each trip?"

"I reckon that depends on how good or bad the fishin' is, Ma. It could be anywhere from one to two or three weeks at a time."

Ma nodded. "I know something has to be done. Do what you think is best."

"Well," Zack answered thoughtfully, "I've been thinkin' about it a lot lately. I really don't see any other way."

"I don't want you to go away, Zack," said Harmony Belle with a frown. "You'll be like Pa, and we'll never see you again."

"No, no," said Zack as he shoved his chair back from the table. Placing a big hand on each side of his little sister's head, he gave her a teasing hair tousle. "I won't be gone that long."

Zack was feeling a little guilty that he had not yet told his mother that he had proposed to Io. Perhaps tonight would be a good time.

After they cleared the table, Zack noticed that Billy Jake went quietly to his room. Before long, Zack followed him.

"Wanna' talk?" asked Zack.

"Don't reckon so," answered his brother.

"You and Billy Joe did a good job tanning that bearskin," said Zack as he stroked the mammoth piece of fur. "It sure looks good hanging here. Why, that thing takes up most of this wall," continued Zack, trying to break the ice.

"I just wish I could've been there when you shot him," answered Billy Jake as he sat up on the bed. "That must've been some sight to see."

"Yep," said Zack. He really wanted to find out what was bothering Billy Jake. "Are you feeling all right, Billy Jake?" he asked.

"I feel all right."

"Well, if you want to talk, I'll be here."

"No you won't," snapped Billy Jake. "You'll be off fishing and having a good time, and I'll have all the work to do around here. You know JJ don't do much unless Ma makes him. I was hoping to keep going to school and make somethin' out of myself. Now I'll just have to be a farmer all my life!"

To Zack, he seemed close to tears. "No. No, Billy Jake," he assured. "If you want to stay in school we'll find a way."

Billy Jake's frown turned into a look of excitement.

"Do you really think so?"

"Sure I do," assured Zack. "You know I got a pretty good education from reading so much and Pa gave me lessons in writing and arithmetic as long as he was around. One of the last things I promised him the night he left was that I would try harder to talk as though I had a better education."

Zack fell quiet for a moment, remembering the pain and fear of that night.

"I have really tried to do better. When Pa was around, it was just like being in school. He had a first rate education, you know. He could have taught in any school."

"Do you miss him, Zack?"

Zack thought for a moment, and then answered, "I reckon I do in some ways, but probably not much. Sometimes he could be really good to be around, but mostly he was mean."

"Yeah, he kept Ma cryin' most all the time," said Billy Jake. "I think we do better when he's not here, don't you?"

"I reckon so," said Zack. "I know the money goes a lot further when he's not here to drink and gamble it all away."

"Yeah, and he ain't beatin' us young'uns all the time, neither."

"You know, Billy Jake, we hardly ever get a chance to just sit down together and talk."

Billy Jake started laughing. "I remember one time we sat down together and was shaking so hard that we couldn't talk."

"Yeah?" said Zack. "When was that?"

"You remember that time we decided to go deer hunting a few years ago?"

"Oh, then!" Zack exclaimed. "Yeah, we were two scared little boys that day. We had a hard time persuading Ma to let us go hunting in the first place."

"Then she fixed us that real nice lunch to take 'cause we were gonna' be gone all day. I still remember what she fixed for us," said Billy Jake.

"It was pretty dark when we left," continued Zack, "and we ran that first mile until we got to the creek. Then we just kept running across it on that big ol' log."

Again they both burst into laughter.

Billy Jake replied, "Big log my foot! We had already run another hundred yards when you stopped and you looked back. Man, you was so scared. You said, 'Billy Jake, do you remember a log being across that creek?' Your legs were just-a tremblin'."

"Yeah," continued Zack, "and then we turned around to go back and see why it was there, and all we found was where that huge 'gator had dragged himself out of the water and disappeared into the woods. I had never seen your eyes so big, and your mouth was wide open."

The brothers laughed for another few seconds then Billy Jake asked, "How big do you think that 'gator was, Zack?"

"He had to have been at least ten or eleven feet to leave a track that deep and wide in the sand, and those foot prints were enormous! Besides that, he reached all the way across the creek."

"Well," said Billy Jake, "that's when we just sat down in the sand by the creek and was shaking so hard we couldn't even talk. That's one time we sat without talking."

"Instead, we got out our lunch and ate every bite," added Zack through his laughter, "then we turned around and came back home."

"Great hunters, weren't we, Zack?"

After a little more laughter, the two fell silent for a few seconds, and then Zack said, "Billy Jake, can you keep a secret?"

"Reckon I can. What secret?"

"Well, I haven't told Ma yet. I've been looking for a good time to tell her, but I'll tell you if you promise not to say anything until after I have a chance to tell her."

"I promise," assured Billy Jake as he crossed his heart.

"Io and me...we're gonna get married."

Billy Jake's eyes opened wide in surprise. "Gosh, Zack, when did this happen?"

"I asked her the day before we went on the bear hunt, and she said *yes*."

"Ma's gonna be real mad that you waited this long to tell her. What do you think she'll say? Do you think she'll say no?"

Zack laughed. "I think she'll be real pleased, Billy Jake. She likes Io a lot, and besides that, I'm eighteen now. I reckon that's old enough to make up my own mind."

"Does that mean you ain't gonna be livin' here anymore?"

"I haven' figured all that out yet. We still have a few more months until Io finishes her teacher's schooling."

"Well, all I can say is that you better tell Ma soon, like tonight."

"I'll try to, but right now I just want you to get back to your jolly old self," answered Zack as he left the room.

Harmony Belle or JJ had let old Bubba in and he was asleep by the fire as Ruby prepared to add another log. The red and yellow sparks were popping and flying up the chimney with fiery determination every time she twisted the poker in the glowing coals.

"You and Billy Jake seemed to be having a good laugh," she said as she placed the poker back in its stand. "What was so funny?"

Zack broke into a wide grin. "We were just remembering that time we ran across the creek on the back of that big ol' alligator. We were both so scared we didn't even want to go hunting after that."

Ma didn't smile. "Then you always wondered why I never wanted you boys to go into those woods and swamps."

In answer to her remark, Zack gave her a quick hug before he went to the kitchen. He poured hot water from the big tea kettle into the tin coffee pot and then added more wood to the coals in the stove. Before long the pot was boiling. By the time he could open the coffee can and pour several spoonfuls of the dark beans into the grinder, JJ and Harmony Belle were beside him.

"Zack," said JJ, "will you play a game of jacks with us? It's no fun to play with Harmony Belle. She takes too long."

"I do not," whimpered Harmony Belle, stomping her foot. "I can play just as fast as you can."

"I don't think I can tonight, JJ," answered Zack as he smiled at JJ and his little sister. "I have several things to do before I go into town tomorrow,"

Zack put the ground coffee beans into the boiling water. The aroma wafted through the kitchen.

"Can I have some coffee?" asked JJ.

"I want some too, Zack," said Harmony Belle.

"Sure," answered Zack while making sure the brew didn't boil over.

"Get the cups down, will you, JJ? And get one for Ma, too."

The coffee started boiling, and just before it boiled over, Zack set it to the side and poured a cup of cold water into the pot to settle the grounds to the bottom.

"I want lots of milk and sugar in mine, Zack," instructed Harmony Belle.

Zack fixed the beverage for his siblings and then carried a cup of the hot brew for his mother and one for himself into the front room.

"Thank you, son," said Ruby as she pulled a rocking chair close to the fireplace and lifted Charity Storm from her pallet to her lap.

Zack pulled another chair up beside his mother and cleared his throat. He took a deep breath then cleared it again. "Ma, I reckon I need to talk to you about something."

Ruby didn't answer, nor take her eyes off her now nursing baby.

Zack cleared his throat for the third time and said, "I suppose I should have told you before now." He fell silent, stirring his spoon in his cup.

Ruby looked at him and raised her eyebrows. "Go on, Zack, tell me what?"

Suddenly Zack felt like a little boy and really wished he didn't have to tell her.

"Well," spoke Zack hesitantly, "the day before I went on the bear hunt, I asked Io to marry me."

Ruby stopped rocking and Zack felt as though her gaze pierced his very soul. He held his breath for a moment.

"What was her answer?" asked Ruby.

Again, Zack cleared his throat. He had no idea how his mother would take it. "She said yes," he answered.

Charity started to squirm, so Ruby began rocking again.

"This is the second surprise you have laid on me tonight, Zack. Do you have any more bolts from the blue for me?"

"No, Ma," Zack answered quickly. "No, no, I… I'm a…"

"Why have you taken so long to tell me? Did you think I wouldn't approve?"

"No, Ma, it wasn't that at all. I… I guess I just never found the right time."

Zack took a swallow of his cooling coffee, and then continued. "I know you like Io very much, Ma, but I love with her with all my heart." He fastened his gaze on the dancing flames and continued. "She makes me feel so good when I'm around her, and when we're apart, I can't get her off my mind. I think about her laugh, and her love for me. I think about her beautiful smooth skin and long black hair, her dark, piercing eyes, and her soft, warm lips, and …"

Suddenly, Zack realized he was rattling on as though his mother were not there.

When he looked at her, her eyes were twinkling and she was smiling. "Son, I well remember those feelings. Love can be a wonderful thing." She looked at Charity Storm and caressed her new daughter's little head.

"William and I were in love just like you are. Those first few months with him were just about the best time of my life. He wasn't drinkin' or gamblin' or anything else that could come between us. Then, we got into a bad financial bind, and I got pregnant with you, so he went back to loggin'. That's when he started back with his old drinking buddies. After that he seldom had enough money for food when he'd come home. Then he got to doing all those illegal things like he did before he met me. From there he was in and out of prison several times.

"Zack, I guess what I'm trying to tell you is that there are actions that can destroy your love. Your pa became so cruel. Every time he would come in and beat you children and me, a little more of that love died. Now, I'm ashamed to say it, but I don't even miss him."

"Ma, I am so sorry that..."

"Wait, Zack, let me finish. It ain't been that long since you were almost as bad as your pa, except you wasn't quite that mean, but if you had kept on drinking, you were bound to be just like him.

"What I'm trying to say, son, is the only way you can have a long, happy marriage is to keep real close to the Lord, you and Io both."

"Io and I have discussed a lot of these things, Ma. I feel like I have been called to preach some day. I talked about it with Io, and she feels the same way. We even prayed about it with Parson Smith."

"Zack," declared Ruby, "you know I love you and I'll never do anything to keep you from being happy. For a long time now I've figured that you two would end up married. I'm very happy for you."

"Thanks Ma."

"Have you set a date?"

"Not really, but we figure it will be some time next June, right after I turn nineteen. Io will be through school then and she thinks she can get a teaching job somewhere."

Ruby smiled and nodded her approval.

"There's one more thing I want to discuss, Ma. Christmas is just about three-and-a-half weeks away, now. You know I don't want nothin' for myself, but I would like to buy somethin' for Io and the young'uns. That's another reason I want to get started with Mister O'Bannon. At least I could help give the young'uns a little bit of Christmas."

"I've been thinking about that, too," answered Ruby. "Do you still plan to go see him tomorrow?"

"Yes Ma'am," answered Zack.

"Here," said Ruby, "take your little sister to her crib. It's about time for me to put the other young'uns to bed."

Zack took Charity Storm from his mother's arms. "Ma, she's so beautiful. She looks just like you."

Zack felt better, having talked to his mother, and was excited about trying to get a job with Mister O'Bannon.

Chapter Nineteen

A New Job

Zack did not get the early start he had hoped for the next morning. He slept much later than usual, and then ended up doing most of the chores.

When he finished, he hurriedly changed clothes and rode to town.

Mister O'Bannon and his crew were cleaning the fishing boat and repairing the nets. They had docked and unloaded earlier that day.

Where has the morning gone? he wondered.

Zack stood on the dock watching for a few minutes. He had never asked for a job before and wondered if there was a certain way to go about it.

Before long his friend jumped from the boat onto the dock and noticed Zack watching him.

"Howdy, Zack," he called. "What brings you here this afternoon?"

"Hello, Mister O'Bannon," answered Zack. "Actually, I came to see you."

"Sure 'nuf, now?" he said.

"Yes, Sir," replied Zack.

"Well, come join me over here and you can tell me what's on your mind."

Zack followed him to a bench that was in front of the fish house.

"How's that family of yours doing? Your mother and that new sister all right?"

"Yes, Sir," answered Zack, "they're doing just fine, except that we've about run out of money. I figured maybe you'd consider letting me work for you. I… I never worked on a fishing boat before, but I'm strong and I learn real fast."

Mister O'Bannon waited so long to answer that Zack thought he was going to say no. Finally, Zack added, "You don't have to pay me as much as you pay your regular men. I just need enough to keep Ma and the young'uns going and maybe give the children a little Christmas."

"Well, I'll tell you, Son, you see that man getting off the boat right now?"

Zack noticed an elderly gentleman who appeared to be limping, probably because of getting old combined with a life of hard work.

"Yes, Sir," said Zack.

"He taught me everything I know about fishing on this lake. He has been with me since I first bought my boat, but now he is getting pretty crippled up. He said that he will work with me one more week or until I find another hand, but I took him to the doctor first thing after we docked. Ole Doc told him he has to hang it up today, and I promised him I would find someone to take his place before we go back out. I reckon you have come at just the right time."

Mister O'Bannon stood. "When can you start?"

"I reckon I'll be here when you tell me to," answered Zack, as he also stood.

"I plan to be here for church Sunday, and we'll leave out about dawn Monday."

"Thank you, Mister O'Bannon," said Zack as he offered his hand. "This will help me and our family a lot. I really do appreciate this chance. What do I need to bring with me?"

"Just bring several changes of good warm clothes, including jackets, caps and coats. The wind really blows cold out in the middle of the Okeechobee this time of the year."

Again, Zack thanked his friend for this great opportunity, and after proper goodbyes, he untied Betsy from the hitching rail and led her several hundred yards up the road.

Soon he came to the big rock that he and Io had sat on the day he gave his life to God. After tying Betsy to the same tree as he had that day, he walked to the big rock and sat down. As he looked over the vast expanse of water, his excitement grew.

He thought about the beautiful painting of a ship that he had grown up with, and the influence it had on his life. Many times over the years he had imagined that he was working on that vessel. Now he was going to get the chance to experience some of his dreams.

Staring out across the lake, he noticed a vessel not too far in the distance, coming in. He watched with fascination until it eased up to the unloading dock.

I wonder how long they were out? he thought. *I hope they got a good haul.*

Suddenly, someone touched him and he spun around.

"Io!" he said with great surprise and pleasure. "What are you doing here?"

She hopped up on the rock beside him and, to his joy, she sat close. He placed his arm around her and gave her a loving squeeze.

"I come here often when I get out of school," said Io. "It always reminds me of you, but my question is what are *you* doing here?"

"I came to see Mister Harley. I'll start working with him Monday morning."

"Wonderful, Zack," said Io. "But that means you will be gone a long time, won't you?"

"Would you really mind if I am?" quipped Zack.

She dug her elbow into his ribs. "Shame on you, Zachariah Bentley, you know I would mind very much! I will miss you."

She laid her head on Zack's shoulder as he tightened his arm around her.

"I will miss you, too, my precious Io. I'll count the days until I can hold you again."

"Zack, I know this is an answer to your life-long dreams, but it is very dangerous and hard work. I really am glad for you, but you must promise me you'll be careful and not take any foolish chances." Io pulled her shawl closer around her neck. "The wind seems to be getting stronger."

Zack took her chin and gently turned her face toward his. "Maybe this will warm you a little," he said as he kissed her soft, full lips.

For several moments Zack was caught in the ecstasy of tenderness. His passion soared as he again felt Io return his kiss before pulling her lips from him. For a moment they gazed into each other's eyes with heartfelt love, their noses almost touching.

"I love you, Io," whispered Zack.

"I love you, too, my darling," Io returned. "I'm anxious for the day when we can be together all the time."

"I know. So am I"

They snuggled together for several more minutes, and then Io said, "I had planned to see Parson Smith today and talk to him about our engagement. Maybe you will go with me since you are in town."

"I didn't think he came to town until Saturday, and sometimes Sunday morning," said Zack."

"He had a meeting with the deacons last night, and he told me he could see me at three o'clock today."

"It's almost three now," said Zack as he looked at his watch. "Are you sure you want me to go with you?"

"Of course, silly, we'll be talking about your life, too."

They walked to the tree where Betsy was tied. Zack took the reins in one hand and Io's hand in the other as they walked to the church.

Parson Smith was sitting on a back pew waiting for Io. "Good afternoon, children. Come in, come in."

"Good afternoon, Parson," Zack said. "Is it all right for me to join you?"

"That is completely up to Sister Io," he returned. "If she wants you here, I'll be delighted."

"I definitely want him here, Parson Smith," said Io as she took Zack's hand. "He is a part of everything I wanted to talk to you about."

Zack felt his face flushing.

"That's fine," answered Parson Smith. "Let's go to the little conference room. I think that will be much more comfortable."

He stood and led them to a small room that had several chairs crowded around a small table.

"Have a seat and we'll get started."

As they sat down, Io said, "I guess you probably know what we want to talk about. For several years, I have been very fond of Zack, and I believe he has been just as fond of me. Zack has asked me to marry him."

As she hesitated, Parson Smith sat quietly, stroking his beard and waiting for her to continue.

"I wanted to make you aware of our engagement, but more than that, I want your approval."

"Well, Zack," said the parson, "how do you feel about this?"

"About Io? I am very much in love with her and have been for a long time."

Parson Smith smiled. "That's great, Zack, but I meant how do you feel about talking to me about your life?"

Zack felt embarrassed. "I… I think it is a very good idea. I also would like to know your suggestions and have your approval."

"Children," said the parson thoughtfully, "God has a very special plan for every life." He leaned forward. With elbows on the table he placed his fingertips together. "Sometimes we get ahead of Him and make a mess of things, but if we seek His will and then do everything we can to follow it, He will set His approval on us. You need His approval more than you need mine."

"I fasted and prayed about this many times, especially before Zack asked me to marry him, and I feel like I found God's will. When Zack finally asked me, I was ready to say yes."

"How about you, Zack?" asked the parson.

"I never did fast, Parson. I really don't understand what that means, or how to go about it, but I have prayed a lot of times for God to direct my life, and you know I talked to you about maybe preaching some day. I've never stopped wanting to preach. Actually, the desire is growing stronger, but I know I'm not educated enough," answered Zack. "I don't have any problem with reading and arithmetic and writing, but I've had very little real schooling. Pa was an educated man and as long as he was around, he made me study."

"That is easy to remedy, Zack. Have you talked to Io about your ambitions?" asked Parson Smith.

"Yes, Sir," answered Zack.

"How do you feel about marrying a man who wants to be a preacher, Io," asked Parson Smith.

"It is an answer to my prayers, Parson Smith. I have always wanted to be active in the ministry, and I believe that God is setting His approval on that desire," said Io. "I will be finished with my special courses soon, and will be qualified to teach. That should help us make it until Zack get the training he needs for the ministry."

"That's wise," said the parson, thoughtfully. "How do you feel about your wife working to help you through your training, Zack?"

"I reckon I need to know how to go about getting qualified to preach just as fast as I can," smiled Zack. "What would you suggest?"

"There's a preacher in La Belle, a very good friend of mine who has started a ministerial training school of sorts. If you could see your way clear to go talk to him, I believe he would be a great help to you."

"Thank you, Parson. If you give me his address I'll find a way to talk to him real soon," said Zack.

"I'll get it for you, Son," promised the parson as they stood.

"Thank you for seeing us." said Io. "I'm sure we'll be talking to you again real soon, won't we Zack?"

"Yes, definitely," he answered as they stepped out of the small room.

"Parson," said Io, "you never did say you would give us your blessings. Will you?"

"Smiling, the parson took both their hands, placed them together. He closed his eyes and began to pray for God to abundantly bless their ministry together, and give them many souls for their hire. Then he said, "You absolutely have my blessings and I also believe you are in God's will. I'll be praying for you both as well as your families."

They started to leave when Zack turned back. "Pastor Smith, I was not able to come when you had your last baptismal service. I really want to be baptized. When do you plan on having another service?"

"It will be as soon as the water is just a little bit warmer, Zack. I'm glad you understand the importance of this ordinance," answered the parson.

"I imagine it will make me a stronger Christian," said Zack.

They left the church in peace, believing that without a doubt, God was in control of their lives.

Chapter Twenty

Preparing for Christmas

Harley O'Bannon's fishing boat docked late afternoon on the nineteenth of December. Zack was very tired but pleased with the knowledge he had gained while out on the water.

He helped unload the fish and clean the deck.

The crew was laughing and some were boisterous but all were glad to be on land for a few days.

Cookie stepped off the boat right before Zack and waited for him.

"Son," said Cookie with pride, "You sho did *real good* for this to be your first trip. I sho was proud of ya." He said it as though he had previously known Zack.

"Thank you, Cookie," said Zack. "I'd be glad to eat your cookin' anytime."

"All right, son, I'll see you next trip," said the old man. He then walked away chuckling and saying something that Zack did not understand.

Zack had a strange inkling that Cookie had touched his life somewhere in the past.

Mister O'Bannon had said they would not go back out until the second of January.

"Merry Christmas and Happy New Year to each of you," he said with a big smile. "You men did a great job this trip. You all go home to your families and enjoy your vacation."

After getting his pay and thanking Mister O'Bannon for this great opportunity, Zack bent over to pick up his bag of dirty clothes. When he stood, he was face to face with Io.

Surprised, he dropped his bag of clothes and started to hug her, then, realizing he was filthy and smelled like fish he said, "I'm too nasty to touch you, but I sure am glad to see you."

With that Io grabbed him and mumbled something about it not mattering to her and placed a joyous kiss on his lips.

"Uncle Billy Joe has the wagon here to take you home," she said.

"How did you know I'd be in today?" asked Zack.

"We've been here the last three days because I wanted to see you so badly," Io answered sweetly.

They walked hand in hand to the wagon, and after greeting Billy Joe, Zack and Io settled into conversation. They talked about everything from Zack's new fishing experiences to how they planned to spend Christmas.

"If it's all right with you, I'll pick you up tomorrow and you can go with me and the young'uns to cut a Christmas tree."

"Oh, Zack," Io said, "that will be great fun, and I'll bring some things to make decorations for it. The children will love it."

"Good, then I'll be there early afternoon, and yes, they will be delighted."

Zack's aching body made him very happy when Billy Joe arrived at the homestead.

December twentieth arrived with beautiful warm sunshine and a gentle breeze. Zack opened his eyes and thought about the past eleven days that he had spent on the boat. It had been a stressful, though rewarding, time. They had come in yesterday with a huge catch, including some of the biggest catfish he had ever seen. He stretched and then sat on the edge of the bed, thinking about the beauty of the rough water, and how that when they were out in the middle of the lake, no land could be seen, anywhere. At first, it had given him an eerie feeling, but he soon got used to it.

The men he worked with seemed very different than the vile loggers that he and Pa had known. Mister O'Bannon didn't allow any roughness or vulgarity on his boat, although he didn't seem to expect those men who were not Christians to act as if they were. Some of them talked about where they were going and what they were going to do as soon as they reached land, punctuating their conversation with loud whoops and laughter. Sammy, a man in his early thirties, loved to play tricks on the others. Zack liked him but tried to stay away from his pranks as much as possible.

The cook was a jolly black man, with white hair and white beard. Everyone called him *Cookie*. Zack was sure that he had known him somewhere before, but had not been able to remember where. *The way he told me he was so proud of me makes me feel like he knows me, too,* Zack thought. Now, with time to think about it, his mind went back to a time when he and Pa were working in the woods north of the lake. Suddenly he remembered.

"Buddy!" he exclaimed aloud. "Of course, it's Buddy!"

Zack's mind flooded with the memories of a time when he had broken his arm in the swamp. Pa asked the black cook if he would let Zack stay in camp and help him until his arm healed.

The first night Pa was gone, remembered Zack, *I stole a bottle from Buddy's cooking supplies and got dog drunk. He realized I was missing from the camp, and found me passed out in a nearby clump of palmettos. He didn't get angry or fuss at all, but talked to me and told me not to scare him like that anymore.*

Buddy, or Cookie as he was called now, had told Zack a lot of stories about his Mama and Papa being slaves, and some of their good and bad times. Zack had enjoyed listening to him and always had a lot of questions about slavery and the way they lived back then. He also told Bible stories at times, but often he embellished them to make a stronger point. Zack had really liked the old cook, and wished he could have spent more time with him.

I can't wait to get back on that boat after the holidays and see if he remembers me, thought Zack.

After dressing, Zack went into the kitchen and found that the rest of the family had already eaten and were out taking care of the animals. Ruby had left a plate of food on the stove for him, which he quickly devoured.

Going out into the warm sunshine, he found Ruby and Harmony Belle gathering eggs. Ruby had fixed a box for Charity Storm to lie in, and she was looking around contentedly.

"Good Morning, Sleepyhead," laughed Ruby. "Did you rest well?"

"Ma, I slept better last night than I have in a week and a half!" he exclaimed as he hugged Harmony Belle.

"I guess it ain't too comfortable sleeping in a tiny cabin with several other men," mused Ruby. "What do you plan to do today, Zack?"

"If it's all right with you, I thought I would go get Io this morning and take her and the young'uns out to find a Christmas tree," answered Zack

"A Christmas tree," exclaimed Harmony Belle, jumping up and down. "We're going to have a Christmas tree! Can I go, too, Ma? Can I go, please?" she begged, pulling on Ruby's apron.

"Child, you're going to pull my apron right off me. Stop," ordered Ruby.

Harmony Belle turned her apron loose but continued begging and jumping.

"Please, Ma, please?"

"You can go if you'll hurry and find where the hens laid the rest of the eggs."

With that, Harmony Belle grabbed her basket and was soon busy finding eggs. Charity Storm began to fuss, so Zack picked her up and cuddled her. She rewarded him with a smile and a soft little hand on his face.

"Now, don't you go spoiling that young'un, Zachariah Bentley! I'm the one that has to take care of her, and I don't have time pick her up every time she whimpers a little." Ruby tried to sound severe, but her smile told Zack that she was pleased to see his affection for his little sister.

"Take her into the house and I'll be in shortly," said Ruby.

Zack carried the baby inside, and before long, Ruby and Harmony Belle came in with their baskets of eggs.

"Here, Son, let me have Charity Storm while you wash the breakfast dishes. I didn't have time to do them this morning 'cause I was busy rocking the baby." Her eyes twinkled mischievously as she grinned at Zack.

"Is that right?" asked Zack. "And you don't want *me* to spoil her!"

Zack soon finished in the kitchen and went out to find his brothers.

They had finished feeding the animals, and were slowly making their way toward the barn.

"Hi," Zack greeted. "What are you boys up to?"

"We were just talking about Christmas," said Billy Jake. "It don't look like we'll have enough money this year to have one."

"Yeah," continued JJ, "we wanted to at least buy something for Ma and Harmony Belle. It won't be much of a Christmas, will it?"

"Now, you boys shouldn't be thinking like that," said Zack. "That's one of the reasons I've come out here to find you. I plan to go get Io in a few minutes, and when we come back, all of us are going to go find a Christmas tree."

"Really? That will be fun," JJ said as his face brightened.

"Billy Jake, as good as you are at wood carving, you should be able to make Harmony Belle a little animal or something she would like," suggested Zack. "As far as that goes, Ma needs a new wooden spoon. That should be real easy for you to make."

"I reckon I could," agreed Billy Jake. "Do you think she would like that?"

"I know she would," answered Zack, "and Harmony Belle would be real tickled with a little animal."

"What can I give them, Zack?" asked JJ. "I want to give them something, too."

"Just give me a little time to think about it, JJ," said Zack as he went into the barn to get a harness for the mule. "We'll figure something out."

"Right now, how about helping me get Molly hitched up to the wagon," suggested Zack.

"I'll run 'er up," said JJ, breaking into a fast trot.

JJ soon returned with the mule.

Zack had been thinking about JJ's unique musical ability.

"JJ, maybe you can come up with something for Christmas that has to do with playing your harmonica," Zack suggested.

"Like what?"

"I reckon you need to think about it," answered Zack. "You're a smart boy. I know you'll come up with something that everyone will like."

Soon the mule and wagon were one, and after saying goodbye to his mother, Zack pulled out of the yard with the rattle of the wagon and a rhythmic sound of trotting hoofs.

Much to Zack's surprise and delight, Io had met the fishing boat yesterday, so she would be expecting him.

It was a beautiful day and Zack was happy. Mister O'Bannon had paid him the same as the other hands, so he would be able to buy a little something for his family and Io for Christmas.

Before long he pulled into the Seminole village and Io ran out to meet him. There was always a spirit of excitement that seemed to travel with her. Zack wondered if that was just a part of being in love, or if others felt it, also? He jumped off the wagon and gave her a quick kiss.

"Mother wants you to come in for a few minutes," said Io.

They went inside. White Fawn had a delicious dessert made, and she was making a drink out of herbs and honey. Billy Joe was sitting cross-legged on the floor, on the side of a long, low table. He nodded and smiled at Zack who returned the greeting.

"Hello, Miss White Fawn," greeted Zack. "Something smells very good."

"Welcome, Zack," said Io's mother. "We want to take this time to celebrate your engagement to Io, and welcome you to our family."

"Wow!" exclaimed Zack. "I didn't expect anything like this."

"Zack," said White Fawn, "Billy Joe and I want to give you and Io a very special blessing, and also, our family has a tradition of this special dessert and drink to celebrate an engagement. This is not an Indian tradition, but our family tradition, passed down from my grandparents," said White Fawn.

"Zack, you and Io sit here," Billy Joe said as he indicated a space across the table from himself.

Io and Zack sat obediently. White Fawn brought the steaming brew and a serving of the special sweet cake to each of them, and then sat across the narrow table from Zack. She then took Io's hand and placed it in Zack's, and placed hers on top.

Uncle Billy Joe stood, raised both hands level with his head, palms upturned, and began to pray.

"Our Heavenly God, Lord and Father of our Lord Jesus Christ, we come before you now to implore your blessings on Zack and Io. You brought them together according to your plan for their lives, to become one in unity and purpose—that purpose being to spread the Gospel to a lost world.

"We now pray that you will give them an abundance of love, peace and joy in serving you as they love and care for each other. Supply their needs and grant them long life. I ask these favors in the name of Jesus Christ our Savior. Amen"

White Fawn picked up her tea and said "Zack, you will always be welcome in our home."

They enjoyed the delicious food and tea, talking and laughing together.

Soon Zack realized it was getting late, so excusing himself he said, "Io, if we plan to cut a tree today, we'd better be going."

Io stood and reached for a shawl and a large bag. Zack thanked Billy Joe and White Fawn for a wonderful celebration as well as for their acceptance and blessing.

All the way home, Io sat close to Zack but said very little. Her long, shiny black hair bounced with the movement of the wagon. Once in a while, a tiny gust of wind blew the long strands across his face, tickling his nose.

"What kind of tree do you plan to cut, Zack?"

"I just figured we'd see one we all like and get it. Do you have another suggestion?"

"Uncle Billy Joe was telling me about a stand of cedar trees just east of your property. I think I can find them without much trouble," said Io.

"Cedars are nice and full. That would be good."

Harmony Belle, JJ and old Bubba came running to meet them as they pulled up.

"Can we go now?" asked Harmony Belle. "Can we go?"

Io laughed and Zack said, "Sure, as soon as we say hello to Ma."

Inside, Ruby was building a fire in the stove and a large chicken was ready to go into the iron skillet.

"Hello, children," she greeted.

"Hello, Miss Ruby," answered Io.

Harmony Belle watched as Io set her bag in an out-of-the-way corner.

"What's that?" she asked.

"I'll show you what's in there when we get back, sweetheart," she said, bringing a smile of anticipation to the little girl.

"Where's Billy Jake?" asked Zack.

He's out there somewhere sharpening his axe," answered Ruby. "I think that boy has been more excited about this outing than he has been in a long time."

"Well, we might as well go. I reckon that chicken will be done by the time we get back, won't it Ma?" Zack asked with expectation.

"Yes," said Ruby, "if you don't get back too soon."

They started walking east across the pasture.

"Uncle Billy Joe said that we should cross the back pasture fence then turn north."

"I've done that plenty of times," said Billy Jake. "Then what do we do?"

"We go about a quarter of a mile and when we see three big oaks in a row, we turn east again. He said we'll probably have to work our way through a stand of thick brush, but just on the other side is a clearing where we'll find a stand of cedars."

Before long they were through the thick brush and were greeted by the cedars.

"Wow," said JJ. "We sure have a lot to choose from."

They began winding through the trees looking for just the right one.

"Oh, look," Harmony Belle said, as she bent over an eighteen inch seedling. "Zack, this is the one I want. I like this one."

"No, silly, that isn't even a tree yet," said JJ.

"Yes it is! This is the one I want," she contended.

"Come on, sweetheart," said Io. "Let's see what else we can find."

"No," answered Harmony Belle with fists on her hips, "I want *this* one."

"Billy Jake," called Zack. "Come cut this tree for your sister."

Billy Jake stepped from behind a large clump of trees, ready to swing the axe.

"What tree?" he asked.

"That one," laughed Io, pointing to the little seedling.

"Whatever you say," said Billy Jake, striking one ground-level blow at the little tree.

Harmony Belle was delighted as Billy Jake picked up the tiny plant and handed it to her.

"You have to carry it home," he instructed, knowing its prickly leaves would constantly stick her.

"How about this one?" called JJ.

They made their way around a few more trees and found JJ standing beside a beautiful, full cedar about eight feet tall.

"The bottom part is a little ragged, but we can cut it about here," said JJ as he pointed to a limb about two feet above the ground.

"It suits me if it's all right with everyone else," said Zack.

"Looks good to me," said Billy Jake. "Where do you want me to cut it?"

"Cut it close to the ground, and we can figure out where we want it cut when we get home," instructed Zack.

After a few well-placed blows with the axe, the tree fell.

"We'll take turns dragging it home," said Zack. "I'll go first."

As they stepped onto the porch, the smell of food whetted their appetites.

Ruby had set the table and was finishing the chicken gravy. The baked sweet potatoes looked delicious.

"That didn't take long," commented Ruby as she pulled a pan of hot biscuits from the oven. "I reckon you got your tree."

"Sure did, Ma," bragged JJ. "It's one I picked out, and Billy Jake cut it down."

"Yeah," quipped Zack with pretended indignation, "and I carried it home. I offered to take my turn first, and that first turn turned out to be from where it was cut, all the way to the house!"

Harmony Belle was waiting patiently for her brothers to stop laughing and talking so she could talk.

"Look, Ma. This is the tree I picked out." She held the little seedling up for her mother's approval. "Isn't it beautiful? I want to decorate it myself."

"Oh, my," exclaimed Ruby. "That is wonderful. What are you going to decorate it with?"

"I don't know. Io," she asked, "will you help me find something to decorate it with?"

"Of course, Harmony Belle," Io answered.

"Dinner's ready," called Ruby as she put the final bowl on the table.

After they gathered around, Ruby said, "This is a very special time for me. Io, it has been hard for me to realize that Zack is grown, and now here he is planning to get married. I just want you to know that there is no one on earth that I would rather have for a daughter-in-law than you."

"Thank you, Miss Ruby," said Io as she hugged her.

Ruby continued, "We don't have much except this homestead that God has blessed us with, but we always have those things that we need to survive. I just want you to know that anything we have, we will gladly share with you. Welcome to our family, Io. Now, Zack, please say the blessing. "

Zack prayed, thanking God for the food, for his mother and family, for his new job and for Io.

"Everything looks so good," said Io.

"Yeah," said Billy Jake. "I'm starving. And by the way, Io, I'm glad you're gonna be my sister-in-law."

"Me, too," said JJ.

"What's a sister-in-law?" asked Harmony Belle.

"That's a woman who marries your brother," explained JJ.

Harmony Belle was too occupied with her drumstick to continue the conversation.

After a delicious meal, Billy Jake excused himself to go make a stand for the tree.

"Will you make one for my tree, too?" asked Harmony Bell.

"Sure, hand me your tree," he said.

This was the first time since cutting it that she had been willing to part with the little seedling. She even held the prickly thing in her lap while she was eating.

Io helped Ruby clear the food and dishes from the table, and then said, "Zack, while you help your mother with the dishes, I'm going to show Harmony Belle and anyone else who wants to join us, what I have in the bag."

She set the big bag on the table and Harmony Belle hopped onto a chair beside her.

"JJ," she said as she pulled colorful scraps of paper and cloth from the bag, "can you get some scissors?"

"Are we gonna' make tree decorations?" questioned JJ.

"That's right, JJ, would you like to help?"

"Sure would. I like to make stuff," he answered as he left to find scissors.

Zack watched as Io got some flour in a small bowl and poured water in a little at the time stirring to get all the lumps out. Soon it was a soft consistency, perfect for glue.

"You are very good with the young'uns," he commented.

Io just smiled and went back to helping the children make decorations.

Soon Billy Jake came in dragging the cedar tree, which was now about six feet tall. He had cut the trunk very straight across and nailed two pieces of wood, cross-fashioned on the bottom. He had also cut and nailed four braces on it. "I don't believe it will fall over," he said as Zack examined his handiwork.

"Looks good to me," said Zack. "Have you decided where to put it?"

"I'll ask Ma," he answered.

Soon Billy Jake had the tree in place and hurried back outside.

Zack finished the dishes and sat at the table to help Io and the children.

By late afternoon, they had a gorgeous array of delicate decorations finished.

Io pulled a skin pouch from her bag and said, "If you will get a large pot with a tight-fitting lid, we can pop and string some corn."

JJ jumped up to find the large iron pot.

"Zack, if you don't mind, stoke up those coals and put some wood on them. It needs to be hot to pop this.

"I'll do anything for you, my sweetheart," he said as he opened the stove and placed another chunk of wood in it.

It didn't take long for them to hear the corn popping in the iron pot. When it stopped, Zack poured it into a large bowl and set it in the middle of the table. Io and JJ began stringing it into long strands of garland.

The night was just falling as they finished and Io said, "I should be going home now, Zack."

After a lot of *goodbye, thank you,* and *it's going to be so pretty*, Zack helped Io into the wagon.

Although the ride home was slow and quiet, Zack thought that if his excited, pounding heart could be heard, it would be ringing a melody through the trees.

They stood together outside Io's home, locked in a silent embrace.

"It won't be long until we won't have to say good night, my darling," said Io.

"It seems like a long time to me," answered Zack. "I don't want to let you go."

"I plan to see you Christmas Day."

"Wonderful," said Zack.

"Your mother asked my mother, Uncle Billy Joe and me to come for supper Christmas evening. If we can find the time, maybe we can make plans for our wedding while we're there."

"That will be great," said Zack.

After one more kiss, Io went inside and Zack drove the mule back home, believing he could really hear beautiful music ringing out from the dark woods.

Chapter Twenty-One

Christmas, 1919

On Christmas morning Zack arose with the sun. He dressed and quietly went into the front room with his arms loaded.

They had decorated the tree with the paper decorations and strings of popcorn. Ruby had enhanced it with the few fragile, dainty glass balls that she had collected over the past few years, and a beautiful glass star for the top.

Sitting on the little table, right beside the big tree was Harmony Belle's diminutive cedar seedling. They had decorated it with very petite ornaments, which Io had made especially for her.

Zack had bought Harmony Belle a delicate China doll wearing a long pink satin dress with several rows of white lace around the bottom of the skirt, neck and sleeves. He leaned the dainty treasure against the wall beside her little tree.

If that little girl asked Io once if Santa Claus would come to our house, she must have asked at least ten times, remembered Zack. Zack chuckled as he imagined how she would act when she saw the presents.

He noticed that sometime, after everyone was in bed, Billy Jake had slipped in and placed the gifts he carved for the family under the tree. Zack picked up the wooden spoon. It had a smooth, perfectly shaped bowl and an extra long handle. He was amazed at the craftsmanship his little brother demonstrated, and the speed with which he had accomplished his work. Zack was sure Ma would be very pleased and surprised. Billy Jake had made an excellent sling shot for JJ from handsome hardwood. This was surely much more difficult to work with but it was not likely to break any time soon. He then saw the life sized baby bunny rabbit that must be for Harmony Belle. The long ears and even the little teeth made it very loveable.

Zack was proud of his brother. He was well aware of his talent, and that's why he bought him a complete carving set which he placed inconspicuously toward the back of the big tree.

For JJ, he had a baseball and glove, and for his baby sister, a rattle.

Zack had wanted to get something special for his mother, so he bought a fancy bottle of perfume and a silk scarf with delicate tatting around it.

Io's gift was still in his room. He planned to give it to her that night.

Ruby walked quietly in. "Zack," she whispered, "what are you doing up so early? I thought you might sleep late this morning."

"Merry Christmas, Ma," he replied. "I got up to get my gifts under the tree before the young'uns woke up."

"It is a pretty tree," Ruby noted. "That was sweet of Io to help the children make decorations. I like her and her family a lot, Zack. Billy Joe has always been here for me and you children when we needed him, unlike yo…" She broke her words but Zack knew what she was thinking.

"We are blessed to have that kind of friends," she finished.

Zack smiled his agreement to his mother's words.

"Merry Christmas again, Ma, and yes, we are very blessed." Zack looked back at the tree and then said, "I'm glad Io and her family are coming for supper tonight. Io and I are going to plan our wedding and set a date sometime after supper. That reminds me, what do you want me to do today to help?"

"I plan to use my one and only white linen table cloth. It's been packed away so long that I almost forgot I have it. Your pa gave it to me right after we were married," said Ruby. "You can get it out for me and iron the wrinkles out."

Zack knew she had it but he had forgotten.

"Oh, Ma," he objected, "you know I always get the iron too hot and burn everything or don't get it hot enough and leave wrinkles. I think you'd better iron it, but I'll get it out for you."

"I'll go take care of the animals. Just let me know if the young'uns get up while I'm out."

"I will," promised Ruby.

Zack hurried through the chores making sure each animal was properly fed and cared for. He took an extra couple of minutes to pet and talk to Betsy. She rubbed her head against his arm as if to tell him how much she appreciated him.

He went back inside and was surprised that the children had not yet awakened.

Ruby was almost finished with breakfast.

Zack poured water into the wash pan and rubbed his hands with the lye soap that he had helped make. After drying his hands, he set about to help with breakfast. Before they could finish he heard JJ coming into the living room.

"Come on, Ma," Zack said. "We can eat breakfast after the kids see their gifts."

"It'll all be cold by then," objected Ruby.

"That won't matter at all," said Zack as he took her arm and steered her toward the door.

Just as they entered the living room, Billy Jake and Harmony Belle came in from the hallway. Immediately, Harmony Belle saw gifts under the tree, and began squealing and dancing around saying, "Santa Claus did come! Oh, look, Ma, Santa Claus came to our house."

Then her eyes fell on the china doll that Zack had carefully placed by her little tree. "Oh, look! She is beautiful. Is she mine?"

Before Ruby or Zack could answer, she picked up the doll and hugged her tightly. She danced her little bare feet around to each member of the family to let them see what Santa Claus had left for her.

"Why don't you sit down right there and see what he left for everyone else," suggested Ruby as she offered her a footstool.

Billy Jake started handing out the presents that he had carved.

"Billy Jake," exclaimed Ruby, "did you really make this all by yourself? It is so perfect! You couldn't give me anything I would like better," Ruby said with delight.

As he gave JJ his sling shot, he said, "JJ, I wanted to make a yo-yo, too, but I didn't have enough time."

JJ took the present with a big smile on his face. "You knew how bad I wanted this. All the ones I tried to make would split. This is great! Thank you, brother."

"What did you make for me, Billy Jake?" questioned Harmony Belle.

"Girl, who said I made anything for you," he teased. "Maybe I forgot you."

Her lip protruded and began to quiver. Tears filled her big eyes before Billy Jake could stop her.

"Oh, Harmony Belle, you know I could never forget you." He sat on the floor and pulled her onto his lap, hugging her.

"Here," he said as he pulled the little bunny from behind him. "How do you like this bunny? Will he do?"

"Yes, yes!" she exclaimed as she examined the beautiful carving. "I love him. I think I will name him Jake because you made it." She jumped up and took it straight to her mother to show. "Look, Ma, he has teeth and big beautiful eyes and Billy Jake made it just for me!"

Billy Jake stood and hurried to his room and then came back with a lovely foot stool that he had made.

"This is for you and Io, Zack," he said. "I started making it the day you told me that you and Io were gonna' get married. I figured you might get your own house some day and you'd need furniture."

"This is really something," said Zack. "This is a good start for our home. I know Io will always love it just as I do. Billy Jake, I am so proud of you."

"Well," said JJ, "now I will give you my presents. He took several sheets of paper from his pocket and passed them out. Each of them looked the same.

On them, he printed:

THIS IS A TICKET TO A SPECIAL PERFORMANCE
PLAYED ON THE HARMONICA
BY JESSE JORDAN BENTLEY
THE WORLD'S GREATEST MUSICIAN
It will be after supper on Christmas night
I will play any song you request (if I know it.).

"Wow," exclaimed Billy Jake, "I know you have been playing a lot lately, but I didn't know you were practicing for a show."

"This is wonderful, JJ," complimented Zack. "Do you have tickets for Io and her family, too?"

"They're right here," he answered proudly, pulling three more tickets from his overall pocket.

"Let's go eat breakfast before it gets any colder," suggested Ruby.

"Wait, Ma," said Zack, "I haven't finished giving my presents yet."

He reached behind the tree and got several items out.

"This is for you, JJ," he said handing him the baseball and glove.

For a moment Jesse Jordan seemed like he would cry. Then he said, "I sure didn't expect anything like this, Zack. I really do like it."

"Since you're so good at carving…," Zack said as he gave Billy Jake his gift.

"A carving set!" Billy Jake exclaimed. "A real carving set! Now I don't have to carve everything with my old knife. I can do really nice work with this. Thank you, Zack."

Ruby turned toward the kitchen.

"Wait, Ma," called Zack, "I'm not through yet. I have a rattle for Charity Storm, and here," he said, handing his mother a package that the woman at the store had wrapped for him.

"Zack," said Ruby, "you shouldn't have spent your money on me."

"Just open it, Ma"

Ruby tore into the white paper and began to exclaim. "Oh, this is the most beautiful shawl I have ever seen." She then saw the luxurious perfume bottle with a fancy atomizer and caught her breath. "It's been years since I've had perfume." She opened it and smelled, then let each of the children smell.

"Son, this was very thoughtful, but you really shouldn't have."

She then looked admiringly at the little yellow and white rattle with flowers painted around it. "I'm sure Charity Storm will learn to love this rattle."

While enjoying a leisurely breakfast, Ruby gave each person chores to get ready for supper guests.

The day hurried by and Zack helped every way he could. Of course, his mind was on Io and what she would have to say about wedding plans. He worried about having enough money to give her the kind of wedding she deserved. Tonight he would give her the pretty little engagement ring that he bought for her Christmas present.

He had also bought a shawl for White Fawn. It had tatting around it similar to the one he gave his mother, and for Injun Billy Joe, he'd purchased a nice hat.

Zack was happy that he could buy these gifts, but knew that from now on he would have to save as much as possible.

JJ and Harmony Belle had never seen Ma's beautiful white tablecloth before. They were accustomed to the red and white checkered oilcloth, purchased at the local hardware. After listening to them, and occasionally enjoying a good laugh, Zack was glad that they could get all their remarks about it out of their systems before their guests arrived.

"You poor little waifs act like you never saw a linen tablecloth before," Ruby chided playfully as she set her prettiest oil lamps on each end of the table and then lit them.

"Well, Ma," said JJ, "Aunt Rita has tablecloths on her table sometimes, but they're not as pretty as yours."

"Thank you," answered Ruby. "Just make sure you don't spill anything on it if you can help it. It's really hard to get spots out of this white linen."

"I'll be very careful, Ma," promised Harmony Belle.

"Me, too," said JJ.

Buddy started barking, so Zack went out to meet their guests. He helped White Fawn down from the wagon as Io alighted in her own nimble fashion.

Harmony Belle ran out squealing non-stop, and grabbed Injun Billy Joe by the hand. "Come in, Injun Billy Joe," she invited. "I want to show you our Christmas tree. Me and Io and JJ made pretty decorations with color paper and she made glue from flour and Ma put a star on the very top and we popped popcorn and..."

By the time she stopped jabbering enough to catch a breath, she had pulled him past the rest of the family and was standing in front of the tree.

"See," she said, "I told you its beautiful!"

"My goodness," Billy Joe exclaimed. "Io told me your tree was a little bitty one. This is a very big tree."

"Oh, yes, here is my tree on this little table. Io made the star for the top of it and I love it, and Santa Claus came last night and left me this beautiful doll and I think she…"

"Harmony Belle!" called Zack with emphasis. "You haven't even given anyone else a chance to say hello."

"That's all right," said Billy Joe. "Little girls this age are supposed to be excited about Christmas. And how are you, Miss Ruby?"

"I'm doing just fine, Billy Joe."

"Is the baby asleep?" asked White Fawn. "It has been a while since I've seen her. I'm sure she's really growing."

"It's time for her to wake up," answered Ruby. "You can go get her if you would like to."

White Fawn disappeared into the hallway while Ruby, Io, and Zack put the rest of the food on the table.

By the time they were ready for everyone to be seated, White Fawn reappeared, holding Charity Storm. She had dressed her in a colorful Seminole outfit.

"Oh, look!" exclaimed Ruby. "That is the sweetest little dress I have ever seen. Just look at all those bright colors. "

"That's the Christmas present I made for her. I was afraid it might be too big but she has really grown."

"It fits her perfectly," said Billy Jake.

"Yeah," added JJ, "with her black hair and all those colors she looks like you, Miss White Fawn."

Everyone laughed.

"Well," directed Ruby, "Billy Joe, you and your sister sit there, and Io, you sit by Zack." The other children had already been told where they would sit, and Harmony Belle's seat had a large pot turned upside down for her to sit on.

Ruby asked Zack to say the blessing. It was a short prayer as he was a little shy about praying in front of others, and beside that, he was hungry, and figured everyone else was, too.

Ruby's efforts seemed to be appreciated by all as the main conversation had slowed dramatically so they could relish her cooking.

All of a sudden, JJ said, "This is the first time Ma's ever used this tablecloth since I was born. Ain't it pretty?"

Before White Fawn could answer, Harmony Belle chimed in, "You and Injun Billy Joe, and Io mustn't spill anything on it because the spots are very, very hard to get out."

Ruby's face turned beet red as Io and her family laughed heartily.

Ruby opened her mouth as though words were coming out, but none did.

"I promise I will be very careful, sweetheart," Io laughed.

"If we do spill on it, we'll help you get the spots out," laughed White Fawn.

"I apologize for their rudeness," Ruby said humbly.

"I thought it was wonderful," said Billy Joe. "It is delightful to sit at a table with children again. We so seldom get to."

The next few minutes were very pleasant as they ate and talked. Often the conversation was in acknowledgement of God's many blessings during the past year. They even touched on the way God had spared their lives when the outlaws invaded their home. They could have all been killed had He not protected them.

Finally Ruby sighed and said, "Those are thoughts I have trouble with so I think I'll change the subject if that's all right with you. Is everyone ready for dessert?"

After unanimous nods, she began dipping blackberry cobbler into small bowls.

"Yummm. Ma, this is really good," complimented Billy Jake.

"Miss Ruby," said White Fawn, "You must teach me how to make this. I make a blackberry dessert, but it is nothing like this. I make an Indian version the way my mother taught me."

"I'll be glad to, White Fawn," said Ruby. Then, standing, she invited, "Let's all go into the front room. I think we'll be more comfortable."

Zack stood and held Io's hand, restraining her as everyone else left the room.

She gave him a questioning look, but he said nothing until they were alone.

"I have been waiting for this all day," he said as he wrapped her tight in his arms and kissed her soundly.

"Zack!" exclaimed a surprised little girl's voice from the doorway. "I'm going to tell Ma!"

"Wow!" said Io beneath her breath as she smiled at Harmony Belle. "Was that kiss supposed to be payment for helping you wash the dishes?"

"Not really," said Zack. "In fact, we are going in there with everyone else. I just want you to know how much I love you."

"I love you, too, Zachariah Bentley," she said returning his affection.

Zack picked up his little sister, and he and Io walked hand in hand into the front room.

Io sat on the home-made sofa and placed Harmony Belle beside her. Zack went to the tree and took a wrapped gift from under it. "Here, White Fawn," he said. "This is for you."

"For me?" she said with surprise. "Zack, I really did not expect you to give me a gift," she continued as she ripped into the white paper.

"Oh, Zack," she said, "I have wanted a dressy scarf like this for a long time. Thank you so much. Just look at that beautiful tatted lace."

She stood and, going to Zack, gave him a hug.

"You're welcome, White Fawn," he said. "I figured we might not be able to do anything next year if I am preparing to go into the ministry. I'm sure that schooling will cost a lot, and I don't want Io to have to start to work until she absolutely has to. Next Christmas might be slim."

Zack then handed Billy Joe an unwrapped hat.

"My goodness, Zack, I'm the last person you should be buying for, but this is a great hat." He placed it on his head and turned around as if modeling it.

Billy Jake reached down and picked up the footstool that he had already presented to Zack, and gave it to Io.

"I made this for you and Zack," he said with pride. "I hope you like it."

"Like it?" exclaimed Io with amazement. "I think it is just stunning! Just look at the shape of the legs and you even made these little feet on them. How did you ever get all four legs shaped just alike?"

"By measuring," he answered, matter-of-factly.

Zack pulled a tiny box out of his pocked and handed it to Io.

She looked at it and smiled. "What's this, Zack?"

"Open it," he answered.

When she opened the small box Zack took out a simple gold ring with a small but brilliant stone in it and put it on her finger. She seemed overjoyed as she showed it to everyone in the room. She then sat down by Zack and, taking his face in her hands she kissed him squarely on the lips.

"Ma," Harmony Belle gossiped, "Zack was kissin' Io in the kitchen."

"You little tattle-tale!" laughed Zack, feeling his face turn red.

"Now," announced Ruby, "If I can have your attention, JJ is going to give you his Christmas present."

JJ handed Billy Joe and the two women the tickets he had made for them.

"My, my!" said Billy Joe. "I didn't realize you played a harmonica. How long have you been playing?"

"I reckon since Pa gave this one to me a couple of years ago. I'll play some songs I like to play," he continued, "and then I'll try to play the ones you want to hear if I know them."

He played several patriotic, church and Christmas songs, and at times they all joined in singing. The concert was crowned with JJ's special rendition of *Silent Night*, which they sang together. Thunderous applause and vocal laurels proved the success of JJ's thoughtfulness.

White Fawn said with tears in her eyes, "JJ, I don't think I have ever been given a more thoughtful gift."

JJ threw his shoulders back and proudly grinned.

Ruby excused herself to put Charity Storm in bed.

"Zack," said White fawn with honest sincerity, "we are so proud to have Io marry into this wonderful family. We realize that no family is perfect and we certainly don't expect it, but you have so much love for each other, and love is the glue that holds any family together."

Billy Joe thought for a moment, and then said, "I know from past conversations with you that you worry about how others will see you because of your father. I don't want you to ever give that another thought as far as we are concerned. You must remember, though William is your earthly father, you are now a brand new creature in the sight of God and in our sight, also. You are a child of God. His Word tells us, *Old things are passed away and, behold, all things are new.*"

"Everyone has sinned," he continued, "but now we are forgiven."

With those words, Zack tried to answer but all he could do was grip Io's hand and swallow back tears. He was glad when Ruby returned.

"Billy Joe," requested Ruby as she handed him their large family Bible, "would you please read the Christmas story for us? That is one of our traditions."

Billy Joe opened the big Bible to the story of the birth of Jesus and again they were reminded that Christmas is all about the greatest gift of all–God gave his only Son to die for the sins of all mankind.

He closed the book and said with a happy smile, "I'm so glad he included Indians!"

"Harmony Belle, it's about time for you to go to bed," Ruby said.

Harmony Belle's lips protruded in a pout.

"That won't do you any good," said her mother as she laughed at her. "It's getting late and you've had a wonderful Christmas day."

Ruby waited patiently as Harmony Belle made rounds hugging guests and brothers amid excited jabber. She tried to relive every moment of this wonderful Christmas day as she made the circle.

With her very active daughter finally in bed, Ruby returned, so Zack and Io slipped off to the kitchen to talk.

"Have you figured out when you want the wedding to be?" asked Io.

Zack thought for a moment. "I think that if we wait until I'm nineteen, that will give me a little more time to save some money, and also, you'll be finished with your special training. That would give you time to plan for the kind of wedding you want. Also, you could probably get a good teaching position by then if that's what you want."

"That makes a lot of sense. I can finish school and still have a couple of months to work on our wedding. Oh, my darling Zack, I know that seems right, but I feel like that is such a long time to have to wait. I want to be with you every minute."

"I feel the exact same way, sweetheart, and I'll accept any date you set. Just tell me when."

While Zack was talking, he gently led Io onto the back porch. Then they walked around the house and sat on the front porch steps where Zack so often went to think.

Bubba followed and lay on the porch beside Zack.

"I don't want a fancy wedding, Zack," whispered Io, "but I would like to combine some Indian and American tradition. Of course, we have a lot of friends and I know they want to be there."

Without answering, Zack showed his agreement by holding her close. He thrilled as he felt her heart beating against his chest until he could not tell which beat was his own.

Inside the house came smooth soft tones of *Silent Night*, as Jesse Jordan again blew harmonic strains of the much-loved carol.

Zack and Io gazed in silence at a heaven full of stars, twinkling high above the Everglades. A falling star swept diagonally across the vast, dark sky, punctuating the beauty of a truly magical Christmas night.

As Zack embraced his incredibly gorgeous and delightfully alluring bride-to-be, he realized that God had bestowed upon him a most magnificent Christmas gift. 'Glades Boy was ecstatically happy.

T. Marie Smith

A 'preacher's kid', Marie lived in several states from Florida to the great northwest. She is an ordained minister, specializing in Chalk-talk evangelism, and has served as a graphic designer for various international TV ministries.

Smith has published poems, short stories, and co-authored and published a novel, **'Onesimus'** with her father, Rev. E. E. Coleman. Growing up listening to his tales of the Everglades strongly influenced her to write **'Glades Boy'**.